P9-BZJ-682

30 FOR A HARRY

Also by Richard Hoyt

DECOYS, A John Denson Mystery

A John Denson Mystery

By Richard Hoyt

M. EVANS AND COMPANY, INC.
New York

Library of Congress Cataloging in Publication Data

Hoyt, Richard, 1941-
   30 for a Harry.

   I. Title.   II. Title: Thirty for a Harry.
PS3558.0975A613   813'.54   81-7847

ISBN 0-87131-357-X   AACR2

Copyright © 1981 by Richard Hoyt

All rights reserved. No part of this book may be reproduced
or transmitted in any form or by any means without the
written permission of the publisher.

M. Evans and Company, Inc.
216 East 49 Street
New York, New York 10017

Design by Diane Gedymin

Manufactured in the United States of America

9 8 7 6 5 4 3 2 1

For Steve Sanger

The newspaper in this story is fictional. There once was a *Seattle Star,* begun in the late nineteenth century by the E. W. Scripps newspaper chain, but that paper went out of business in 1947. The writers, editors, and publisher in this story are also fictional. They are not intended in any way to resemble journalists associated with Seattle's two current newspapers, the *Times* and the *Post-Intelligencer.* The same is true of the issues in this story. There was a Harry Karafin. In 1967, Karafin, then fifty-one and a respected investigative reporter for the *Philadelphia Inquirer,* was exposed as having used his position to extort Philadelphia area businesses. *Inquirer* editors were forced, in print, to call their employee of twenty-nine years "a remarkably adept shakedown artist." How did he do it? the editors asked. Their answer: "Gall. Cruelty. The Big Lie."

1

I LEARNED TWO THINGS of value in my newspaper days. The first is the motto of the country: *ubi est meum* (where is mine?). The second is that everybody has a story. The stories are comic, poignant, tragic. You make of them what you can. If you have the stuff, you survive. If you don't, you drink too much. In the detective business, people and their stories can suck you in and draw you on. Their stories hurt. They can kill.

The woman with the blouse had *ubi est meum* written all over her face. That and more.

She was dressed to provoke. Her black slacks came from an aerosol can. The buttons on her transparent blouse were undone to her sternum. She had large breasts on a slender torso; her nipples pushed provocatively against the fabric. She had a body that would bend like a reed.

You don't find women like that in Pig's Alley. I hang out there because the Pig's has a couple of dart boards up and because the vegetable market on Pike Street is next door. Darts is a civilized game. There is just no possible way to get irked at somebody who beats you at darts. You just lose, that's all. When you win, you thank the gods your stroke was on. When you lose, you shrug it off.

I go there every Friday to throw darts, drink beer, and watch people.

That Friday the Pig's had a thick-fingered black man with tiny yellow eyes and no neck playing the upright, a Baldwin so old the veneer was peeling on the sides like sheets of dried mud. The cornet player pretended he was Louis Armstrong and wrapped his instrument in the same handkerchief he used to blow his nose. The drummer, a white man in a black man's game, was numb from coke. There was a yellow plastic bucket if you wanted to contribute.

She watched me walk in the door. Watched me pause to check out the dart boards which were being used. She grinned when I stopped at her blouse. The women in the Pig's tended to worn jeans and conversations about ex-husbands, Alice B. Toklas, and cosmic orgasms. This one was different. Ask me my story, her eyes said.

Well, I'd pass. Only get myself in trouble. "A draft and a hot dog, please, Wally," I said to the bartender. The woman with the blouse was disconcertingly close; I could smell her perfume when I left for a table.

She came right on along.

When a woman like that comes right on along it's a bad omen.

"May I join you, Mr. Denson?" she said. She was as sleek as a greyhound.

I looked up at her, my mouth full of hot dog, my eyes full of nipples. "I'm a sport," I said.

"You are John Denson, the detective?"

"Oh, yes. That's me."

She sat and started to say something but was interrupted by the waitress, an earnest young woman named Flora who was dressed for either fashion or protest, I wasn't sure which.

"A Budweiser, please," said the woman with the blouse.

"And another hot dog, please, Flora," I added.

"My name is Samantha Becker," my new friend said when Flora left.

It was hard to keep my eyes off her chest. "The hot dogs're my dinner. You got my name from?"

"Wally, the bartender."

"Ahh." I didn't believe her. I'm not a hunchback, so women don't run the other way. I'm not Robert Redford either. Women like Samantha Becker don't ask bartenders for my name.

Samantha looked uncomfortable when Flora delivered her Budweiser without a glass, but she didn't object. "I was talking to Wally about you before you showed up. He said you have an interesting background: a former newspaper reporter, a former intelligence agent. He said you write, too."

"Wally tell you all that?"

"Well, some of it." She smiled.

"This doesn't look like your kind of place, Ms. Becker. I come here for the jazz and to watch druggies and derelicts. Why are you here?"

"You, Mr. Denson. I came in here for you. I'm told you come in here just about every Friday night." She chased a gold chain around her throat with her thumb and forefinger. When she reached the insides of her breasts she turned her hand and lazily stroked the skin with the edges of her fingernails. She watched the people on the small dance floor.

The jazz was slow and bluesy. The folks at the Pig's were going at one another in slow, randy grinding. The cornet player was a sheen of sweat; he looked like he had been stoking pig iron. Great purple veins bulged in his neck as he tried for more decibels.

"Would you like to dance, Mr. Denson?"

"The name is John. Sure."

What she did when we got to the dance floor would have been called statutory rape fifty years ago. I liked it a lot but had sense enough to know she was after something. Whatever it was, she wanted it badly. She wasn't shy; she began chewing on my neck for warm-ups.

"Say, just what is it you're after, love?" I asked her ear.

She leaned back and gave me a smile. "Why don't we go back to my place? We can talk about it there."

If experience told me to back off, my hormones wouldn't have any part of it. "Why can't we talk about it here?"

She grinned. "More fun there."

"Why don't we talk about it at my table?" I paused. "For starters, that is."

9

"For starters," she said.

She followed me back to my table, where I ordered another draft beer from Flora. "The deal is you order draft beer and you get a glass," I told Samantha. "Do you want to talk to me on a professional matter?"

"Well, yes."

I smiled. "I should tell you from the start I don't work for free."

"It doesn't have to do with me exactly, Mr. Denson."

"What does it have to do with?"

Samantha Becker looked at the band then back at me. "It has to do with you and a client."

I sighed. "It's against professional ethics to talk about another client's business."

"You never break that rule?"

"Never."

"What if we just went to my place to talk it over? You won't have to discuss it with me if you don't want to."

"I can't even confirm that I've been hired by any particular client."

Samantha shook her head. "What if you're being used and I could help you out?"

"If someone is using me, I'd like to know how, sure. You'd never use me though, would you?"

She paused. "Well, maybe a little. But we can hardly talk about that here with the music and all, can we?"

"I agree. We go to my place, though, not yours."

We got back to my place and settled down in bed with not a whole lot on, and Samantha Becker picked up the conversation.

"Now then, you first," she said. "I want you to tell me."

"Me? First what? I don't have anything to tell."

She moved my left hand onto the inside of her thigh. "Sure you do. I want you to tell me what you're going to do on that fishing trip. What's his pitch? What did he tell you? Do that and I'll tell you what you should know."

"What if I told you I don't know what you're talking about?"

She moved my hand a trifle higher. "I'd say you're a liar and not a very good one at that."

"Fishing?"

She studied my eyes in the dim light. "We'll talk about it in the morning." With that and by way of shutting me up, she moved my hand all the way; we didn't talk about it anymore that night.

In the morning she was gone. I wasn't surprised, but I did wonder what she was after.

I spent the whole day scrounging through city directories in the Seattle public library. I was trying to trace a father who had ducked out on child-support payments. When I got back that evening a letter was waiting for me, slipped under my door:

Dear Mr. Denson:
    You may regard the enclosed $200 as an advance of sorts. If in the end we decide not to do business, it's yours. There is a cafe named the Hungry Coho on the wharf at Ilwaco. Please be there at 5 A.M. Monday. We'll cross the bar for a try at the salmon and discuss our proposition there. This is a confidential matter; please keep this note and your trip under your Stetson. Discuss it with no one.

There was no signature.

There are usually two reasons why prospective clients go to such lengths to preserve their anonymity. For some, those on the very precipice, it means confessing some personal, wounding hurt. Going to a private detective is like going to a priest. For others, trapped by circumstance, it means risk. A matter of the heart in the first case. Usually a matter of the wallet in the second.

This one could be either.

On some matters the police just aren't any good. Cops don't understand passion or don't want to. And if the law is involved, they don't have to understand; they're protected by the appropriate statutes, neatly numbered, carefully worded, awaiting the lawyers.

I put the letter on the windowsill, tipped my chair onto its rear legs and opened a Rainier. There's nothing better for thinking than city lights and a cold beer. The girl across the way hadn't put on one of her dramatic exhibitions for several days. I could see the flickering blue of her television set beyond the opaque yellow of her drawn blinds.

Those with apartments on my side of the U-shaped apartment building had a view of the Sound. I liked to watch freighters being guided into the harbor and the ferries coming from the Olympic Peninsula. The ferries arrived every thirty minutes and on a night like this looked like something out of a Fellini movie: vast, gay ships crowded with people full of hope and eager for a good time, sliding through the fog and cold rain of the Puget Sound. There was a ferry arriving below; the lights on deck twinkled and blinked in the grayness. The people on the ferry were on their way to the Kingdome; the Seahawks were playing an exhibition game against the Atlanta Falcons.

I took a second look at my letter. Whoever wrote it knew how to get my interest. It was written on newspaper copy paper and the writer had tightened each sentence with a pencil before he mailed it. Editing can become compulsive, like a nervous tic, for people who make their living on a typewriter.

First Samantha Becker, now the note. It seemed like everybody in town knew what was going on except me.

Why would anyone want to see me on a fishing boat? I didn't care why; the silvers had been running for weeks and the papers said the chinook were beginning to move.

2

I HAD BREAKFAST in a place called Kate's on Ilwaco's single street, which leads inland from the boat harbor. Kate's sold box lunches for $2.50. I bought one of those too. Not bad, had two generous sandwiches, one ham, one beef, and a banana. It was 4:30 A.M.

The residents of Ilwaco really only have a four-month year —from June through September, when the salmon are running. The rest of the time they mend their boats, stare at the rain, dig razor clams when the tide is right, and wait for the fish. The silvers—or coho as they are also known—actually make their appearance in late May, but the fishermen don't begin arriving in numbers from Seattle and Portland until June. The real fishing, for the enormous chinooks, doesn't take place until late August and early September. While silvers run from six to twelve pounds, a chinook will start at fifteen pounds and run as high as forty or fifty pounds.

The harbor itself is sheltered from the **Pacific Ocean** by a peninsula that contains a coast guard station, lighthouse, and park. The park has the inevitable hookups for recreational vehicles. RVs the folks call them. They are evidence, at one and the same time, of people's inability to disengage themselves from a television set and their preference for fondling machines rather than one another.

One side of the U-shaped harbor is flanked by a row of restaurants, bars, gift shops, and fish canneries where you can swap your catch for canned salmon. Behind commercial row and to one side of Ilwaco's single street is an enormous parking lot. It is still dark when the fishermen arrive. The only sounds are of automobile engines, car doors and trunk lids being slammed, men coughing and blowing their noses. Then they gather on the wooden boardwalk that flanks the harbor below to wait for the lights to appear, one by one, on the charter boats. To a man they were thinking, although few would admit it, that this was the *day,* their day, the day they would catch the big one. It could happen to anybody. Why not them?

I bought a Styrofoam cup of coffee from the Hungry Coho and went outside to meet my shy client. It was cold but there was no wind, which was a good sign. Heavy seas on the bar can have everybody heaving his guts out in minutes. I waited about ten minutes before I got a tap on the shoulder. It was a kid of about sixteen wearing a rain slicker and a pleasant smile. He would be the bait boy.

"Mr. Denson?" he asked hesitantly.

I tried a W. C. Fields. "Ah, yes, my boy, the very same," I said, watching him over the rim of my Styrofoam cup.

I don't think he knew W. C. Fields from Wallace Beery.

"Our party tells me you're their guest this morning. You're in luck, the fish were really hitting yesterday. They tell me the boats averaged two fish a client."

Boy did I ever know that story.

"What's your boat's name?"

"*Papa's Ark.*"

"And how did the *Papa's Ark* do?"

The boy looked chagrined and shrugged his shoulders. "Damned near got skunked," he grinned.

"What's your name?"

"Bristol."

"I'll tell you what, Bristol. I'm not paying for this trip so I don't especially care. I've spent a lot of hours on the water

14

trying. I can tell you that even if a chinook went out of his way to hook himself, if I'm holding the rod I'll come up with some way of losing him."

I followed Bristol down a wooden walkway to where the *Papa's Ark* was moored. Bristol scrambled on board to help the captain get the gear squared away. I went below to meet my client.

Clients, I should have said. There were two of them in their early sixties, looking uncomfortable as I found a place to sit down.

"Gentlemen," I grinned expansively. "Helluva day for fishing, eh?"

They were obviously not fishermen. The older was dressed like he was trying out as a Ringling Brothers clown. He wore black-and-white tennis shoes that were obviously borrowed and too large for him, a pair of well-worn Pendleton wool slacks, and a bright red nylon windbreaker that was brand spanking new.

He cleared his throat and extended a soft hand, which I shook. I grinned, narrowed my eyes, and sized them up in a caricature of movie detectives. "And your name?"

He hesitated. "Balkin. Harold Balkin. But I must repeat that this meeting absolutely must be held in the strictest confidence."

"John Anders," said the second, and he too shook my hand. Anders watched me with wary blue eyes above a cigar, which he shifted nervously in his mouth.

He was built like a blocking back on a single-wing football team. He was short, broad-shouldered, and in his day would have been quick and tough. But he had gone to gut somewhere along the way and now looked like a refrigerator with legs. He obviously felt foolish dressed up in a borrowed fishing outfit. He pulled at his nose.

Balkin was owner and publisher of the *Seattle Star*. Anders was the newspaper's editor in chief, no doubt the one who had written the note to me.

The big diesel of the *Papa's Ark* loped into a throbbing idle the first try; Bristol unfastened the deck lines with a flourish. We were under way. The citizen's band radio was on. It

15

wouldn't be long before we would be hearing gossip about the hot spots. It was unstated but understood among the three of us that this wasn't the time to begin our business. We would watch the captain negotiate the narrow channel that led into the broad mouth of the Columbia and the bar just off the peninsula that protected Ilwaco from the high seas and heavy wind.

We had no sooner left the harbor than the captain, a large man named Bernt Johansen, came below to tell us his plans. He squatted and put a palm on the deck for balance.

"We'll be going out about ten, maybe fifteen miles. That's where the action was yesterday, in fairly deep water. It'll be an hour, maybe an hour and a half before we do any fishing."

Johansen suspected we had something to talk over. He was telling us this was our chance.

"I think we'll get some action today," he said. He retreated to the deck, where Bristol was rigging the gear.

It was Balkin who spoke first when Johansen had disappeared. Balkin was in charge.

"Mr. Denson, we asked you to come here today because you were a newspaper reporter before you turned to the detective business. You were, as we understand it, a good one."

"I was a good writer but a fuck-off," I said, and gave him my self-deprecating grin.

Balkin closed his eyes for a moment. He had no doubt been warned.

"Yes, we got that impression also." Balkin smiled.

That one simple gesture told a lot about Balkin. Ever the gentleman.

"We talked to Bernstein about you," said Anders. He shifted the cigar in his mouth.

"Bernstein!" I started to giggle.

"Bernstein said you were maybe the best writer he ever had but you had a penchant for smart-ass leads. Had to watch you like a hawk."

Bernstein had been my city editor, an egomaniac who loathed women reporters and dull stories. He was impossible to get along with but I liked him. I could see him now looking across the city room at me with those small, gray eyes and that

16

awful beak of a nose. Bernstein liked me, too, and invariably gave me the best story of the day. Bernstein knew why I quit. We had the same problem, which was why he'd never go far. The interests of his readers came first. He was a professional and everyone knew it. Not long after I left, he was purged from the city desk.

"He tell you about the turd in the punchbowl line?"

Anders shook his head. He'd had people like me on his staff before.

"Did you ever hear the story where Bernstein yelled 'fuck' fourteen times while he threw handfuls of press releases around the city room because the guy on cops missed a story?"

Anders shook his head again but started to grin. Maybe he wasn't all bad.

"Bernstein was a trifle hard to get along with but he was a good man," I said. "Knew a story and could write."

Anders leaned forward. "Mr. Denson, have you ever heard of a man named Harry Karafin?"

Of course I'd heard of Harry Karafin. "Late of the *Philadelphia Inquirer*," I said. I knew at once the awful, sickening reason why I had been chosen to rendezvous with these men on a fishing boat.

Anders said nothing.

"If you have a Harry Karafin on your staff I'll pin him," I said. I like newspapers a whole lot. If Balkin and Anders had had their reservations about me a half hour earlier, they were now visibly relieved.

Harry Karafin, it should be noted, was an investigative reporter for the *Inquirer*. Harry leaned on corporations for a few spare bucks in exchange for not printing damaging stories in the papers. It all went well, what with Buicks, summers in Europe, and furs for the wife, until a magazine in Philadelphia blew the whistle on him. It had been a trifle embarrassing to the *Inquirer*.

To all the honest and honorable newspapermen out there trying to do a job, the very idea of a Harry Karafin is outrageous. A decent newspaper such as the *Star* could hardly afford to have a Harry on its staff.

Balkin crossed his legs, so the incongruous tennis shoes

took stage center in the tiny cabin. "We don't know that we have a Harry on our hands, Mr. Denson. We only suspect it."

Suspect, my ass. Samantha Becker and whomever she was working for didn't suspect anything. They knew damn well I was going on a fishing trip with the editor and the publisher of the *Star*. When she found out I hadn't been asked yet or wasn't going to talk, she got the hell out. She was either a pro or well coached.

"Mr. Denson?"

I snapped out of it. "Sorry," I said. "I was just thinking. Who is your Harry?"

It was a question that had to be asked. These two men were the brains behind a large, well-edited metropolitan newspaper. They were proud of the *Star* and the people who put it together each day. Now this. It was one thing to go to the elaborate precaution of meeting me in secret on a fishing boat. It was another to actually name the Harry. It was like confessing a case of the clap to your wife.

The big diesel was pushing the *Papa's Ark* along at a brisk clip. I could see the skyline of the Oregon shore receding. The Douglas fir on the coast range was at first green, then blue, now blue gray, and would soon disappear entirely.

"Wes Haggart." It was Anders who said it.

I was surprised and it showed. Wes Haggart was considered an ace reporter. Solid in every respect. "Jesus Christ!" I said.

Anders closed his eyes and shook his head. "I know. I know. I know. Wes Haggart of all people."

I knew they must have something solid to go on to pursue it this far. I asked the next question: "What makes you think so?"

Balkin seemed suddenly aware of his tennis shoes. "These skis belong to my teenage son. My wife insisted that I wear them so I wouldn't slip on deck. The reason, Mr. Denson, is that an acquaintance of mine, who owns stock in both the *Star* and several other corporations in Seattle, suspects it strongly. A warehouse belonging to a subsidiary of one of his companies burned to the ground under mysterious circumstances. The insurance company investigated and refused to pay. The parent company was naturally chagrined and put the chief executive of their subsidiary on the line. He said he paid a bribe to keep the story out of the *Star* until he could sell his stock."

"Wes Haggart covered that story?"

Anders nodded his head yes. "Not a hint of arson in his stories."

I thought about that. "How did he manage to keep it out of the other paper?"

"I don't think it's any secret that Wes has lots of contacts with the police. I'm sure it's no secret that he scratches backs with the cops all the time. If he got to it first I'm sure it wouldn't be that tough."

"Anything else?"

Anders rubbed his eyes and said, "Yes, Wes drives a Mercedes Benz sports car and owns a luxury condominium. How many reporters do you know who drive Mercedes Benz sports cars?"

I had to laugh at that one. "Maybe he plays the ponies," I said.

Balkin looked at me evenly. "This is no laughing matter for us, Mr. Denson. I'm sure you appreciate our situation."

"Your situation is that if Haggart is a Harry, you want to pin him yourself. You want to hand the case over to the cops with everything in place. Then Mr. Anders here will write an eloquent front-page editorial informing your readers that the *Star* found its own cancer and got rid of it immediately. But if you don't do that . . ." I paused.

Balkin raised his eyebrows.

Anders cleared his throat.

I continued: "Then the County Prosecutor, Roy Hofstadter, will flail you unmercifully with your Harry and use it to become governor like he wants, a distasteful prospect since he's built his career on baiting the press."

Balkin looked resigned. He crossed his legs and batted nervously at an incongruous tennis shoe that had taken stage center. "I'm afraid that's all true, Mr. Denson, but unfortunately there's more to it than that. We can certainly endure a little embarrassment. If we lose circulation we'll gain it back eventually. And even if Roy Hofstadter should be elected governor and make life harsh for us, that too would pass."

I couldn't imagine what he was talking about. That was no doubt made clear by the expression on my face. Bewildered. Typical John Denson.

"Mr. Denson, what do you consider the top three metropolitan newspapers in the United States?"

I paused for only a second. "The *New York Times,* the *Washington Post,* maybe the *Los Angeles Times.*"

"And they have what in common?" Balkin leaned forward in the tiny cabin.

"Hell, I don't know."

"Take a guess, Mr. Denson."

Anders relit his cigar, which had gone out. He watched me intently, as did Balkin.

"Well, they try to do a fair and complete job of covering national and international news . . ." I started to continue but Balkin stopped me short.

"No, no, we know all that. I mean what is it that makes them superior newspapers? What sets them above run-of-the-mill newspapers and chain-owned newspapers?"

"The commitment of the Sulzbergers, Katharine Graham, and Otis Chandler."

Balkin grinned. "Precisely. They're family-owned newspapers. And the families that own them take pride in their quality. They're willing to pay well for the best writers and editors. My family, the Balkin family, has owned the *Seattle Star* since the nineteenth century just as the Ochs and the Sulzbergers have guided the *New York Times.* We're not the *Times,* but we do the best we can. Good newspapermen around the country know that."

The *Papa's Ark* plunged into a rough set and Balkin almost lost his seat. Anders held on and bit viciously into his cigar. I rolled with the motion and wondered what Balkin was getting at.

He got right at it: "The problem is that newspapers have become large corporations, and fewer families have the resources to compete. And right now, as you know, we're in the

20

middle of a costly technological revolution in which a new generation of machines comes along every three or four years. The computers promise to save enormous sums in the long run, but in the short run they're costly as hell. We have to buy them to stay in business."

"Which has what to do with Wes Haggart?"

"Are you familiar with a gentleman named Tobias Lane, Mr. Denson?"

I slumped visibly. Tobias Lane owned the second largest newspaper chain in the world. Balkin and Anders looked out to sea.

"Shall I continue, Mr. Denson?"

"Please do." I wasn't sure I really meant that.

"As you may know, newspaper chains control roughly 70 percent of the daily newspaper circulation in the United States. Although there are a few decent ones, most chain newspapers may be graded bad and worse. Tobias Lane's chain, which has more money than its executives know what to do with, is one of the most rapacious. It markets newspapers the way McDonald's sells hamburgers. In Lane's view, owning a newspaper is a license to print money; copy is the stuff you use to fill the space between the ads."

"You're trying to tell me that if Roy Hofstadter finds out Wes Haggart is a Harry, then the *Seattle Star* will somehow wind up in the hands of Tobias Lane and his crew?"

The inelegantly dressed publisher of the *Star* winced and looked me in the eye. "That's almost precisely on the mark, but you should know the details."

I waited but nobody said anything. "Well?" I said at last.

Balkin toyed with the band of his wristwatch. "Why don't you tell him, John? You know the story as well as I do."

Anders regarded the ash on the end of his cigar. "The *Star* has been owned by Harold's family since 1892."

I was impressed, and my face showed it.

"They've always had a son or daughter who liked newspapers. That's what it takes to publish a decent newspaper, not a sheet."

"What happened?"

"Over the years the stock became dispersed among more

21

and more members of the family, with two exceptions: Harold and his sister, Ruth. She's his half-sister, really, and is twenty-two years younger—which would make her what, Harold?"

"Forty-one," said Balkin.

"Harold owns 35 percent of the *Star*'s stock. Ruth owns 25 percent. Until recently a number of cousins on the maternal side of the family owned the remaining 40 percent. About ten years ago Ruth married a high roller named Andrew Trotter who proceeded to squander her money on half-baked schemes. She divorced him a couple of years ago but was stuck with enormous debts."

"*Ubi est meum*," I said.

"What?"

"Nothing," I said. "Continue, please."

"It was then that our friend Tobias Lane began buying off the cousins one by one. None of them really gives a damn if the *Star* is a quality newspaper. They have friends who own stock in newspapers who are making a hell of a lot more money than they are. They wanted to know why."

I stopped him with my hand. "Let me guess. Lane told them it was Harold's fault, that he was spending too much in the newsroom and on unnecessary machinery, and in the end they bought his story."

The memory was apparently still painful for Balkin. "Listen, Denson, we're right square in the middle of switching over to a computer-operated VDT system. That costs money; there's no way around it. I tried to explain, but they wouldn't listen. Sure, it will cost money in the short run. But in the long run we'll save hundreds of thousands of dollars in back-shop labor costs. But all they did was complain that their income is down. They just didn't give a damn about the future and never have."

"And Tobias Lane kept tantalizing them with suitcases full of greenbacks," I said.

"The son of a bitch," Balkin muttered.

"So he now owns 40 percent of the *Star*."

"He owns 40 percent and after he gets to Ruth he'll own 65 percent," Balkin said.

"How long can she hold out?"

"I'm not certain, but if what I hear is true, not much longer.

Ruth worked on the *Star* as a reporter for eight years, but all that's in the past now. I don't think she cares one way or the other anymore."

I guess I never will understand the ways of families. "Don't you talk to your sister, Mr. Balkin?"

Balkin smiled. "Not for four or five years now. I opposed her marriage to Trotter, but she wouldn't listen. She's hated me ever since. Seattle is a small town, Mr. Denson. I think I have a fair understanding of her financial position."

"What you're saying is that if Wes Haggart is a Harry and your circulation takes, say, a six-month dive, your sister, Ruth, won't have any choice but to sell to Tobias Lane."

"That's it precisely," said Anders. "They'll send out a bunch of kids from the East Coast to tell us how to do business. They'll still be picking pimples, for Christ's sake, but they'll try to tell us how to publish a newspaper in Seattle, Washington. They have nimble fingers on a cash register but that's all; the hell with the readers."

Balkin looked out the window like he'd just discovered there was an ocean out there. "Tobias Lane is not, under any circumstance, to know we have this problem with Haggart. Not under any circumstance, is that clear?"

"That goes without saying."

"If that happens, we might as well throw in the towel."

"I'll have to start by talking to your source," I said.

Balkin looked at me like I'd beaned him with a fastball. "No," he said.

"Well then, how do you propose that I get the stuff on your Harry, if he is one?"

"That, Mr. Denson, is what we're paying you for. You've worked a beat. You know how to ask questions."

Anders interrupted in an effort to help his publisher out. "We propose to put you on the payroll as a reporter. We'll call you an 'investigative reporter' and let you pursue the same kinds of stories as Haggart." He smirked. Investigative reporter was a two-bit term used mostly by professors of journalism.

I looked at Balkin. "You know the first thing I'll do is read the fire clips for the past year and go from there."

"That's what I'd do," he said.

23

"What if I get close to your source?"

"I've talked about that with him. If you get close, I'll arrange a meeting. Until then, he insists on anonymity. Given his circumstances, I can understand why."

Samantha Becker remained. She knew about my fishing trip before I did. One of these gents was a liar or had fucked up.

"How many people on the *Star* know you might have a Harry on your hands?"

"The two of us," said Anders.

"No one else?"

"No one."

I looked at Balkin. "Are you sure?"

"I've told no one. I assure you."

"How about your wife or secretary?"

"Not either."

"You obviously don't usually go salmon fishing. What was your pitch there?"

"Both our wives and secretaries think we're attending a reception given by the *Vancouver Sun*. They've installed some new equipment up there and want to show it off."

They both seemed honest enough, threatened by the possibility of having a Harry on their staff. If one was a liar, however, I couldn't challenge him here. Do that and I'd lose my advantage.

"Good," I said. "We'll have to keep it that way. I don't want you to make notes. Don't discuss it on the phone. I'll keep in touch in a way that's safe."

"Done," said Balkin.

"How about you?"

Anders nodded yes.

"What else do I have to worry about?"

Anders sighed. "Powell."

"Ah, yes. The good Charles Powell." Powell was the *Star*'s city editor, a misanthrope with a reputation that rivaled Bernstein's at the latter's most tyrannical. I puffed my cheeks full of air and let it out slowly.

"How do I get along with Charley?"

"Can you write a lead?"

"Depends on the story."

24

"Charley Powell's a lead freak. He'll either like you or think you should be fired. It all depends on the first lead you give him. If it's good, you'll have no problems. It it's wordy or dull you're screwed."

"One lead, just like that?"

"Just like that," said Anders.

"What if I draw a Rotarian speech?"

Anders smirked. "Then you're in a heap of trouble. What he'll do is come running to me brandishing the offending lead, tell me you're bush, and demand we get rid of you before you make the Guild probation."

"Christ, you can't zap every poor bastard who draws a lousy story."

Balkin, who had previously been rescued by Anders, returned the favor. "I'm afraid what John says is true. And we have let go of an extraordinary number before they made probation. Some of them went on to first-rate papers, the L. A. *Times, Miami Herald.*" His voice trailed off, and he pulled at his nose.

I'd always wanted to ask an editor straight out why he puts up with a raging jerk as city editor. I had my chance now and I wasn't going to let it pass. "Why," I addressed Anders, "do you people make city editors out of the Bernsteins and the Powells of the world?"

Anders regarded me thoughtfully. "A good question, one I expect you've always wanted to ask a man like me."

He was clairvoyant. "That's it on a dime," I said.

"Some, as you know, become city editor by kissing ass. All editors and managing editors are partial to that, myself included. It's a quality that loses its charm after a time. Others are solid newspapermen; that's true of Powell and I suspect of the legendary Bernstein as well. The job makes them what they are. There's no worse job under the sun."

It was true. What he said was true. "Were you ever a city editor?"

Anders grinned. "I married the daughter of the editor of the *Boston Globe.* Yes, I was a city editor for four years."

"I certainly hope you haven't told Charley Powell about your possible Harry."

He laughed. "No way. You can bet on that. Incidentally, the staff is engaged in a little game with Powell. They do their damndest to give newcomers a good story, hoping one day to slip an incompetent by him on the basis of one lead. If he gives you the ding, I'll simply overrule him."

I shrugged my shoulders. "It shouldn't make any difference anyway: it sure as hell won't take me four months to find out if Wes Haggart is a Harry."

Balkin cleared his throat. Under all that charm there lurked a cash register. "About your fee, Mr. Denson?"

I tried to look charming, modest, and self-deprecating before I stuck it to him. "The way I see it, if Wes Haggart is a Harry and I pin him before Hofstadter, it will be worth maybe several hundred thousand dollars to your corporation, not to mention saving the *Star* from Tobias Lane. Add to that an impossible combination: I'm a detective, an experienced reporter, and I know Seattle. It should take me two, possibly three weeks at the most. Under those circumstances, twenty-five hundred a week plus expenses is peanuts."

I felt my heart thump. I'd never earned a fee like that in my life.

"Done," he said without hesitation.

And I knew I'd blown it. I should have asked for twice that. I was sick. What a jerk.

Balkin knew what I was thinking: "Cheer up, Mr. Denson, you can always pad your expense account."

"I'll bet you never told anybody that before."

"That's the first time. Your job won't be easy."

At that point Bristol the bait boy came down the narrow stairway to tell us that we were at yesterday's hot spot.

He had thawed out some frozen herring. Each fish got two hooks, one through the snout and the other through the back. Once in the ocean, the herring flashed convincingly through the water. A live herring probably wouldn't get worked up, but salmon were capable of being fooled. The herring were taken deep by a plastic disc that acted as a foil.

We didn't talk any more business after the fishing started.

We took only one fish and that was mine, a twelve-pound silver. Anders was a competitor and was pissed that he didn't

26

get one, but considered it a betrayal of his position and status to let it show. I don't think Balkin really cared. He seemed amused that his colleague took it as a failure. When Balkin wanted salmon he went down to Pike's Market and bought himself one.

It wasn't the best start. Things wouldn't get better.

3

IT WAS A FINE, crisp Seattle morning and a good day to start a new job. I was about a half block away from the entrance to the *Seattle Star* when I saw someone I knew on the sidewalk ahead of me.

Samantha Becker. Dressed in a classy suit.

Samantha was with another young woman. They had apparently gotten off the same bus. They paused in front of the entrance of the *Star*; Samantha's friend turned inside the building. Samantha started walking downtown.

I wanted to talk to Samantha, but the other woman promised to be a better prize. The woman, who had light brown hair streaked blonde in front, said good morning to an adolescent with pimples, breezed easily into the anteroom outside John Anders's office, and took a seat behind a desk. She was Anders's secretary. Oh boy!

Wes Haggart should have given her and Samantha better instructions about security. I couldn't imagine he was that sloppy in running his business as a Harry.

Now that I knew who Samantha's friend was, I decided she could wait. Time to go upstairs to the city room and meet the storied Charley Powell.

It was an enormous city room, carpeted and more posh than those in which I had toiled in Honolulu. It looked almost civilized on the surface. Those who have worked in a city room know better. No politics are more awful or debilitating than newspaper politics. Some reporters are favored, others screwed. There are competent editors, illiterate editors, bearable editors, and hated bastards. Publishers generally stay out of sight, but few are known to be other than tightwads and haters of the Guild.

And each day the writers and editors, alcoholic, cynical, and neurotic as they are, do their damndest to make sense out of that vast, fetid tub of manure that is the American city. The people out there are crying, laughing, bleeding, dying, and lying. It doesn't take a reporter long, not long at all, to know the awful, unbearable truth. And so across the land they sit in the bar next door hunkered under the weight of their burden and swap callous, barbarous, outrageous stories of life in the city. These are men who know that God is, in fact, dead.

So it was that I reported to Charley Powell, the man responsible for it all: the city editor, first sergeant of purgatory.

He was a tall man who might be described as cadaverous. He had stooped shoulders, a long face, and straight black hair. He had big black pouches under slate gray eyes. He even looked like Bernstein. He watched me with disinterest as I made my way through the desks. He assumed I was yet another flack with some half-lie I was about to palm off as truth.

Charley Powell knew how to handle a flack. He and his two assistants handled mountains of press releases each morning, more often than not sweeping them off the desk into the wastebasket with one grand, cynical scoop of the arm. So much for that day's horseshit.

"Yes?" He paused, pencil in hand, watching me with eyes that had seen all.

"My name is John Denson," I said.

The pencil lowered. Powell rubbed his eyes. "I think we met before, last winter. You were in here with Phillips on that business with the San Francisco woman. The woman detective."

"The very same," I grinned.

Powell took his hand away from his eyes and looked at

me. "A detective. Tell me, are you related to someone around here? That's a real question."

I shrugged my shoulders. "Not that I know of; I guess you can never tell."

He leaned forward. "Listen, I gotta tell you. Anders never tells me a damned thing around here. All I ever get is bitch, bitch, bitch, we're overstaffed, and now you. It doesn't make any sense."

"What can I say? I got fed up with the private detective business and applied for a job. I gotta eat. The man said yes."

Powell began doodling with the pencil. "Listen, Anders says I'm supposed to give you your head, like Wes Haggart. Does that make sense? I gotta cover a town. I need more Wes Haggarts like I need a hole in the head."

Poor bastard. I understood his problem. "Listen," I said, "if I had my druthers I'd go general assignment, but I think this private detective business went to Anders's head."

Powell's jaw tightened. "Tell me, how do you see it, the reporting business I mean?"

"The way I see it, there are bum stories and good stories, lazy reporters and reporters who work, reporters who can't write and reporters who can."

He grinned. He had it in him. "Well, we try to do a job around here. Do you know what the word *hopefully* is?"

"An adverb."

"That's encouraging. If you want to get along with me I'll never see the words *finalize, innovative, parameters, input, utilize,* or *parenting* in your copy."

"I'd just as soon eat a maggot sandwich and that's the truth."

"And the last thing I'll tell you is that when the President of the United States says 'fuck' in his state of the union address, we'll print it in the *Star*. Not before then, so don't play games."

Another humorless bastard.

But not as humorless as the man who suddenly appeared behind him. This man wore the sterile trappings of a scientist in a laboratory. Only he wasn't a scientist; he was a technician of some sort, a bastard mixture of scientist and bureaucrat. He was a tall man, long-faced, wearing pale blue trousers, shined black shoes, and a white smock. The notebook in his hand matched the blue of his trousers. He was proud of his notebook; it was the sign of his authority.

"We'll be installing three more VDTs this morning, Mr. Powell," he said. It was a statement of fact. The man in the smock represented the inexorable and knew it. He opened his blue notebook.

Powell ignored him and turned to me. "Do you know what a VDT is, Denson? Can you imagine writing copy on a screen?"

"Last sheet I worked on still had Linotypes."

"This is Clifford, Denson."

Clifford said nothing.

"You may not know it, Clifford, but there's a certain sublime pleasure in rolling a piece of paper into a good, solid typewriter." Powell gave his machine an affectionate slap with the palm of his hand.

The tall man opened his blue notebook. "Sign here, here, and here." He pointed with his finger.

Powell was in no hurry.

Clifford waved for workmen in pale blue coveralls to enter the city room. There were three of them, and they had been watching through a glass door. They came on through now, each pushing a dolly loaded with a cardboard carton. "You know where they go," Clifford said to the first man through.

Charley watched the workmen weave their way through the city room.

"The first step was carpets, Denson. Then they wanted to install glass barriers between the desks, said it would give the reporters privacy. The real reason is some asshole couldn't stand the idea of people having a good time while they work. The pay's not that good, Denson. Take away the bullshit and what have you got?"

"Probably figured they could reduce the staff and save a few bucks."

"I think you're right, Denson. What do you think, Clifford?"

"Please sign the form, Mr. Powell."

Powell signed.

31

William Clifford closed his notebook and walked off.

Powell turned to me and blinked once. "First you, now this shit. I don't know what to do anymore."

Powell pulled a crumpled wad of a handkerchief from his hip pocket and blew his nose. "Well, here's the deal. We don't stick anybody with the obits. If you don't have anything to do except pick your butt, grab a handful from that wire basket there and help us out. For now there's a free desk next to that blonde over there, name of Shay Harding. And I wouldn't get any ideas, I think she's dating an obstetrician or some damned thing. I'll talk things over with Anders and get you on a project tomorrow."

"Square," I said. I turned and saw John Anders disappear into the men's room. I followed, ever the casual John Denson, and claimed the second urinal. The room was empty except for us.

I stared straight ahead at the graffiti on the wall. "Say, do you ever make notes to yourself that you don't share with your secretary?" I said.

There was a pause that was a little longer than I expected.

"Please don't make any more, especially about the matter we talked about."

"Did something happen?"

"I can't be sure," I lied. "But if you have to make notes to yourself about the Harry, keep them in your wallet."

"I understand," he said in a voice that sounded sick.

"You left a note to yourself in your desk, right?"

"That's right," he said.

"And you're wondering who could have gotten to it?"

"Right again."

This was no time to encourage panic. "Maybe no one," I said. "And if they did it's not that important. Just don't do it again."

"You can believe it," he said. The *Seattle Star* had a bundle on the line. He paused. "But how did you know?"

"Just believe me, I know."

He zipped up his pants and regarded me thoughtfully before he turned to wash his hands. "Maybe you're not such a flake after all," he said.

32

I followed him out of the john and claimed my desk next to Shay Harding. She was no hard-bitten newspaper broad. No sir! She was five foot seven maybe and so slender as to be almost hipless. She walked with her head up and shoulders back. Her body said she liked herself and felt good. It was a pleasure to see. She had a nice mouth, especially the lips. She had a full, sensuous lower lip. But the most stunning thing about her, except for her smile, was her hair. She had blonde hair that cascaded in great lazy waves six or eight inches below her shoulders. She was obviously proud of her hair and took care of it. I could see her sitting in front of a mirror brushing and counting "98, 99, 100."

But it was her nice smile that took the breath out of me.

"John Denson," I said, shook a soft hand, and stared into extraordinary light blue eyes.

"We've all been wondering if you're related to John Anders," she said. She winked the left blue.

"No truth to that. Charley Powell says you're dating an obstetrician, is that right?"

The blues looked amused. She smiled. Julie Christie. She almost had Julie Christie lips on top of everything else. "Not a chance. Charley's got the horns for me and wants to keep you away."

"Ah, well," I said. "Ladies with looks like yours never had much time for John Denson anyway. I wish it were otherwise."

"You never know. Did Anders warn you about Charley's thing about leads?"

"Oh yes, he told me."

"I thought you might be Denson when I saw you talking to Charley. This is the best I can do." She handed me a note about Pacific Northwest Telephone. It seems people were complaining about suggestive massage parlor ads in the Yellow Pages. Ma Bell was moved to clean up her act.

I read the note. "This their flack's number?"

"Sorry I don't have anything better," she said.

I shrugged. "I'll see what I can do. How will I know whether I've scored?"

Shay put one finely manicured fingernail to her lips. "If you miss, he'll simply pass your copy on to the copy desk without a word. If you score, he'll look at you, look disgusted, and shake his head. If he says 'Oh shit!' you've tripled off the left-field wall."

"You like baseball?"

"Love it."

"How about football?"

"That too."

"Sportswriters stingy with tickets?"

"They're okay."

Shay Harding sounded like my kind of girl. I called the telephone flack and got the details of the massage parlor debacle.

When I had my dope I stared at my machine for a couple of minutes then laid it out:

"Although the massage parlor ads may be the most exciting part of the telephone directory, a stern Ma Bell yesterday took steps to take the titillation out of the pages where the fingers do the walking."

I finished the story and gave it to Charley Powell.

"You should have shown it to me," Shay whispered.

"Just wait," I said.

Powell looked up at me and stared for what must have been thirty seconds.

No look of disgust.

Then it came, followed by a grin and a sad shaking of the head. "For Christ's sake," he said, and passed it on to the copy desk.

"Better than 'Oh shit'?" I asked softly.

"Lower left-field bleachers," she said. "You shoot pool?"

"Not very well, but I don't mind losing."

I did a pile of obits to show Charley Powell that I was a regular guy, then adjourned to the morgue to rummage through fire clips. It took a couple of hours to find the one I wanted. The main warehouse of Fielding Enterprises, a wholesale food company that sold to schools, hotels, and industrial clients, had burned to the ground with a six-month supply of stock. A fireman was quoted as saying that the source of the fire was uncertain; there was no mention of suspicious circumstances or a pending arson investigation.

34

There was a separate bundle of Fielding Enterprises clips. It was a thin bundle but it told me what I wanted to know. Fielding had been in financial trouble for several years. The corporation's executives tried to negotiate a merger with a larger outfit but were reluctant to sell their assets at a loss.

When Fielding's warehouse burned, a sharpie like Wes Haggart should have asked questions.

I wrote a note to John Anders, sealed it, marked it personal, and stuck it in his office mailbox:

> J. Anders:
> I think I tickled Charley P.'s fancy with my first lead so he shouldn't come running. Please tell him you want me to investigate what is apparently a large number of industrial fires during the last year. Tell him the company knows it will cost money but doesn't care; tell him you want this to be a solid job for the reader. Try not to giggle when you tell him the company doesn't care if it spends money. You might bite the inside of your mouth or concentrate on your mantra if you have one.
>
> I'll keep in touch.
Denson.

That chore done, I headed for sports. The editor's name was Walter Proctor. He wrote a daily column. I recognized him by his bald head and wire-rimmed eyeglasses.

"John Denson's my name. I'm new city-side," I said.

Proctor looked up from his typewriter. "Walter Proctor." We shook hands.

"Listen, they put me next to a blonde named Shay. She tells me she's a football fan, and my question is: how hard is it to bum tickets off you guys?"

Proctor grinned and opened his desk drawer. "Not hard at all, but if you're gonna take Shay out, I'd do it on the sly. I wouldn't make book on it but I'd say that Charley Powell regards her with something of a proprietary interest—not that she'd have anything to do with such an obnoxious turd."

"You could take him or leave him?"

"Just as soon leave him is accurate. Thank God I don't have to work under him. You're interested in the 49'ers game next week?"

"It'd be nice."

I got my tickets, forty-five yard line. They weren't nosebleed seats either.

I retreated to my desk. Shay was working on a story about the alleged dangers of microwave ovens. I slid the tickets onto her desk.

"Walter Proctor says if we go see the 49'ers I shouldn't let Powell know."

Her eyes widened at the sight of the tickets, but she didn't say anything for a minute. "The deal is, I think he regards me like a daughter or something. At least I hope to hell that's all. Of course I'll go to the game with you."

"Does Wes Haggart ever drink at the bar next door?"

"Every afternoon."

"How about Charley?"

"Never goes near the place. He'd rather sit over here and brood about the alleged inability of anybody but himself to write a funny feature."

"I think I'll go hide out there this afternoon. When you finish with the apocalypse of microwave ovens you might come over and we'll have a drink."

Shay gave me a nice grin. "If you'll give me a minute, I can come with you now."

I sat down. "I'll wait. You can never tell where something like this'll lead."

"Oh, yeah?" She raised an eyebrow.

"I thought there was something wrong with this place, now I know what it is. It's quiet in here."

"They moved the wire service machines into a little sound-proof room over behind that glass."

I looked, and she was right. There they were going churg, churg, churg in splendid isolation.

"Why did they do that?"

"Anders said management hired an efficiency expert who concluded the racket was distracting. But we all think the reason is that Powell likes to eavesdrop on our conversations and the machines were too much competition."

"Sounds like the cows."

"Cows?" She flipped her long blonde hair with a toss of her head.

"They did a study that said cows give more milk if the barn is wired with Muzak. Do anything for you?"

Shay looked down at her breasts. "I'm not sure I'd be much of a producer under the best of circumstances." She pulled the sheet from her typewriter and studied it briefly. "Finished."

"I don't know how you can think in all this splendid silence."

"It isn't easy." She laughed. She handed in her copy and we headed for the bar next door.

4

THE BAR WAS CALLED "More" after the traditional notation at the bottom of each page of copy alerting the editor that more is to come. Whoever owned it was in the chips. That's true of anybody who owns a bar next door to a metropolitan newspaper. The only trouble with newspaper bars is that flacks tend to hang around like cowbirds trying to impress everybody that they're just folks. Flacks are good for freebies and an occasional favor, but nobody with taste wants to associate with them in his spare time.

I knew there would be several reporters there complaining. Complaining about Powell. Complaining about Anders. Complaining about the weather. It was the same everywhere. Reporters at the *Star* were no different.

Only here the rain really was something to complain about.

There were eight reporters seated around a long table cluttered with pitchers of beer, plastic baskets of popcorn, and ashtrays of smoldering cigarettes. The air was blue with smoke. It was a melancholy group. They stared out of a tinted window at the rain coming down.

Shay glanced at the table with the reporters and went to an adjoining area where there were pool tables.

"Wes Haggart here?" I asked as she racked the balls for stars and stripes.

"Not yet, but he will be. He holds court here every afternoon. You break or shall I?"

Now I'm a darts player, not a pool player. I play darts so I can have a social life. People who bowl or play golf are not my kind of people. I'd never seen anybody like Shay Harding shoot pool before. "After you," I said. I was an awful pool player. Someday maybe I would get to show her the pleasures of darts; right now I was on her turf and pool was her game.

She chalked her cue, which I saw screwed in half at the middle and which she must have brought with her.

"You bring that thing with you?"

"Yeah," she said, and grinned.

"Oh boy!"

Oh boy is right. She put the cue ball to the side and stroked it with a top spin. A wicked break.

I chose a stripe, an easy shot, and missed.

Shay ran the table except for the one ball. It was fun watching her. Anybody can pocket a ball with top spin or backspin. Shay could handle left or right English as well. The trick was in the leave. Shay thought one shot ahead. She would throw her blonde hair to one side with a toss of her shoulders, bend her back like a willow, rump and right elbow up, concentrate on the ball, and stroke her shot with a cue that neither hooked, jerked, nor scooped. Although she probably didn't think of herself as an athlete, she was, and a good one in a sport most people associate with truck drivers and cigar smokers.

I pocketed the fifteen ball, then missed again.

Shay banked the one, called a tough shot on the eight ball, and sank it. She never horsed the cue ball. She used only enough speed to get the job done and give her a leave she could use.

"Another game?" she asked.

"I don't know why not."

"Good," she said, and smiled. She was probably running out of male opponents who didn't resent watching those slender wrists stroke in ball after ball.

I hung in there, doing my damndest to concentrate on the

39

ball, but it was no use. I was always off just a fraction. "Maybe I'm a piss artist," I said.

"A which?"

"That's an English term for someone who can shoot darts when he's drunk. Maybe if we drink enough I'll gain on you."

I didn't gain, and in fact lost four straight before Wes Haggart came into the More. I should say made his entrance into the More. Haggart was a commanding figure, a large, handsome man with a great mane of black hair prematurely streaked with gray. In an age of receding chins, Haggart had a real jaw. There was something vaguely Asian about his cheekbones. He had intelligent green eyes that quickly surveyed the room, sizing up that which mattered and that which did not.

He commandeered the chair in the middle of the table where the reporters were drinking. The man who was in the chair moved without a word. That chair was Haggart's turf. So he sat, with his back to the rain, and his companions were rendered observers.

I tried two more times to beat Shay, but it was hopeless.

"I think it's time for me to go and pout."

Shay looked disappointed. "Does this mean we won't shoot pool anymore?"

"Heavens no. It does mean that I'll probably check a *How to Shoot Pool* book out of the library and read it in secret, like a dirty book."

"I was beginning to get bored anyway," she said. She gave me a smile that said she'd had fun. She unscrewed her cue and put it away in a leather case.

Haggart had apparently learned of my status on the staff. When I was introduced, the green eyes watched carefully, weighing, calculating.

"Pleased to meet you," he said. His grip was firm. I don't think there was any doubt he suspected my job involved more than doing a better job for the *Star*'s readers. But he wasn't sure what. He was wary. He was careful. "We were talking about Watergate," he said. He filled my glass from a half-empty pitcher.

Watergate, long past, is important to reporters in the provinces as well as the big leagues. It is important because

40

the *Washington Post* adhered to an honorable tradition that keeps the hope alive that any reporter might one day be in the right place at the right time. The tradition is that a reporter who stumbles onto a story is allowed to stay with it as long as he does a job. So it was with Carl Bernstein and Bob Woodward, who were covering the Virginia and Maryland suburbs, the Siberia of the *Washington Post*. A high school graduate and a Yalie with a reputation as a bum writer brought down the President of the United States. It is the stuff of myth.

Shay, who had heard it all before, as had I, excused herself to go to the john.

Haggart paused and ran thick fingers through his great mane of hair. I helped myself to some more popcorn and a second glass of beer, communion for a newspaperman.

A thin man named Randolph, who covered courts and who was drunk, sucked a tooth and said, "They didn't send him to jail."

That was the flaw, of course, the blemish on a nearly perfect triumph.

"There may never be another story like it," said Haggart.

I think I understood the reason for his reputation. Haggart had the ego and the sense of moral superiority to tackle anyone in town and bring him to his knees. The only restraints were the corporate interests of the *Star* and the decency and common sense of his editors. Within those limits Haggart was willing to go to any lengths to feed his ego. Other reporters, lesser men in his eyes, had neither his energy nor sense of outrage and were willing to collect their paychecks at the end of the week and spend their time laughing at Woody Allen or kissing women on the neck.

The question was, could this man who strutted and swaggered with his reputation as a fearless seeker of truth succumb to the temptations of a Harry?

I saw Haggart glance at me, trying to figure me out. "What's Charley have you on?" he asked.

"For starters, he wants me to investigate industrial fires in Seattle for the past year. Said hard times have brought a rash of arson problems for insurance companies."

41

"Charley said that?" Haggart poured himself another glass of beer. He was a cool one.

"Any ideas for starters?"

He looked me square in the eye like a hillbilly over five-card stud. "Fielding Enterprises," he said.

I looked right back and didn't blink. Felt like John Wayne. "I saw that stuff in the clips. You think they burned it themselves?"

"I'd make book on it, but you can't get close to it."

"Mind if I have a go?"

Haggart shrugged. "Have at it. If you pull it off, the beer's on me."

If Wes Haggart was a Harry, he was in a jam. He knew why I went fishing. He knew why I was hired. I had made his problem even more clear with my arson lead.

Shay returned from the toilet. It was a distraction which both Haggart and I welcomed. There were too many opportunities for messing up when you're going one on one against a man you think might be smarter than you.

Shay's thigh settled next to mine. I didn't know whether it was there by accident or on purpose. We drank beer. The thigh remained. We talked about the weather. Still the thigh remained.

Then my bladder began to fill as I knew it must. After twenty minutes the pain began to get to me.

"Are you okay?" Shay asked.

The pain whipped through my bladder.

I nodded yes.

"Are you sure?"

My eyes were glazed over; I hated to part with the warmth of her thigh. "I think I'm going to be paralyzed. I'll tell you when I get back." I got up and went to the john.

When I got back the thigh returned.

"Oh, Sweet Jesus," I said.

"What was the matter?" She looked concerned.

I pulled back her brushed blonde hair and whispered in her ear.

"You damn moron." She began giggling, but was flattered.

42

A woman like Shay was enough to make me forget about Wes Haggart, but Haggart had something on his mind. "I suppose we should talk, Denson, you know, about Fielding or whatever." He ignored Shay and refilled my beer glass.

"No sense us chasing down the same leads. I'd rather work with you than against you."

Haggart grinned. "My feelings exactly. Only I don't think this is the place," he said. He looked at Shay, who was pretending to be oblivious to our conversation.

"You name it," I said.

"How about my place, say in a couple of hours? We could have a drink or two, maybe swap old war stories."

"Your place is fine by me," I said.

Haggart wrote his address on a bar napkin and handed it to me. He looked at his wristwatch. "Right now I've gotta be going."

"That'd be about eleven o'clock," I said.

"I'll be there." With that, Haggart left.

Shay was impressed. "Wes Haggart? Inviting you to his apartment to swap stories? That doesn't happen. Haggart works alone. I don't know of anybody who has been up to his place."

"Maybe he's getting mellow as he's getting older."

Shay laughed. "Not Haggart. He wants something."

"From me?"

"From you, Mr. Denson."

"Probably wants to make sure I don't poach on his territory."

"If that was the problem he'd go to Charley Powell. This is a case of Wes Haggart inviting a nothing newcomer up to his apartment."

"Let's drink beer now. I'll tell you all about it in the morning."

I got to Wes Haggart's apartment about five minutes early. The door was open about six inches and I could hear an FM disc jockey explaining a jazz cut by Chick Corea. I maybe should have arrived earlier.

Wes Haggart was slumped across a coffee table, the side of his face in a pool of blood. He wasn't alone. Samantha Becker was on the carpet, minus half her face.

And on Haggart's couch was John Anders's secretary, staring up at the ceiling. She didn't see anything. She was dead.

All three were dead.

I touched nothing, left the door as I found it, and called the cops and the *Star*'s police reporter from a phone booth a few blocks away.

5

THE POLICE REPORTER had plenty of time to meet his deadline. It was all there the next morning—lead story, top right, under a banner.

Wesley John Haggart, thirty-seven, investigative reporter for the *Seattle Star*, had been found murdered in his Queen Anne's condominium. Haggart had been shot twice in the chest by a pistol.

Found dead with Haggart were Leslie Anne Dunham, twenty-five, executive secretary to John Anders, editor of the *Seattle Star*, and Dunham's roommate, Samantha June Becker, twenty-seven.

The story said Samantha Becker was a buyer for a women's clothing store in downtown Seattle.

I reread the story twice, folded the paper, finished my coffee, and drove to the *Star*. I arrived late, and Charley Powell was waiting, one hand on the bridge of his nose, the other holding a cup of coffee.

"We have to talk, Denson," he said quietly.

I saw that Shay was late for work also. "I'll get a cup."

Powell waited, doodling on a press release, while I got my

coffee. Powell studied me carefully as I walked back to his desk. When I sat down, he stopped doodling and dug his thumbnail into the pencil's eraser. "Anders told me yesterday you were an intelligence agent and a private detective in addition to being a former reporter. Is that right?"

I nodded my head yes.

"You know we can't let that bastard get away with murdering Wes and those girls."

"Do we know the same pistol killed all three?"

"Yes. The cops checked the slugs this morning."

"You want me off the fire story."

"I want you off, now. Are you any good?"

"We can all use breaks," I said.

"I want you to find out who murdered Wes and the two girls. I want you to do your damndest to beat the police. Cut any corners you want, I'll look the other way. Work day and night; overtime is no object."

I took a sip of coffee. "Have you checked with Anders?"

"Fuck Anders. When a cop is killed they damned well find out who did it. The same goes for us. I don't care what Anders wants. He can sit on it; I'm city editor of this newspaper."

Yes, he was. And ordinarily his word was law. But there was every chance that Anders and Balkin would want me to keep my distance now that their Harry was dead. They had nothing to gain and everything to lose by stirring the manure. I couldn't tell Charley Powell that; he'd just had a reporter murdered and was understandably enraged. So was I. Charley Powell had to be on my side: there was no other way. I needed three or four bodies involved. If I had, say, Charley and two others on the chase, it would be virtually impossible for Anders and Balkin to stop me.

I moved my chair closer to the edge of Powell's desk.

"Got a few minutes?" I said. "This is a bit complicated."

Powell began making neat circles with a pencil. "I've got all the time it takes."

"I'll give you some background, then I have a bit of a request. You said you were willing to cut corners if it meant finding out who murdered Wes Haggart."

"I said it and I meant it."

46

"This conversation is between the two of us. Our word as honorable men."

"You have mine." Powell took a sip of coffee from his Styrofoam cup.

"Do you know the story of Harry Karafin?"

"The guy from Philadelphia."

"The same."

Powell nodded.

"Anders and Balkin think Wes Haggart may have been another Harry."

"Bullshit!"

"Well, I'm telling you straight, Charley. You have to believe me. Do you keep a flask in your desk?"

"No, but Jenkins does."

"Why don't you fix my coffee?"

Powell removed a pint of Hill & Hill from the desk next to his and more than fixed my coffee. "What do you think of their story?" he asked.

"I think they sounded damned convincing, and what I've found since then doesn't help Haggart's case much."

"Did you ever meet him yourself?"

"I drank a little beer with him last night and I have to go along with you: it's hard to believe. I'd like to have Shay help me out."

Charley half rose out of his chair. "You want to involve Shay in this business?" he asked incredulously.

"Well, there are a lot of things a woman can do that a man can't."

"Like what?"

"There used to be a fat man named Greene, special projects editor for *Newsday,* supposed to have had a sign that says 'If you don't have anything to do, take a banker to lunch today.' "

"What's that supposed to mean and what does it have to do with Shay?"

I shook my head. "Think, Charley. We have two things to find out: if Wes Haggart was a Harry and who killed him. When a man takes shortcuts to make a bundle, he has to put some distance between himself and his wad. That's usually because of our friend the tax man. In this case it would also

47

be to hide it from the owners of the newspaper. Now there are several ways to do that, usually through the use of dummy corporations. A savvy hustler can frustrate damn near anybody trying to trace the bucks. But there has never been a high roller, ever, not one, who did not have some way arranged to get at his money."

Powell thought about that. "Hence the banker."

"But there's not a damned thing the banker can say legally."

"Ahhh!" Powell grinned.

"Comes the blonde. A little hip here, a smile there, we have our dope."

"How do you know that's the case here?"

"I don't yet. Even if it doesn't come to that, there's a lot of legwork I need done."

"Next you're gonna tell me you two work real well together."

"Well, there's that." I grinned. "Also I need one more body, a man, older, not married. There may be, uh, some quasi-legal work involved."

Powell squinted. "What do you mean 'quasi-legal'?"

"I mean illegal."

"What kind of illegal?"

"I don't want to tell you."

"Of course you'll tell me, or I won't get one of my reporters involved."

"What you don't know won't hurt you. Like I said, I need a single man and he'll have to agree to it. Also, I'd appreciate if you didn't tell Shay just yet. I may not need her."

Powell stood up. "I gotta think. Taking a hike for coffee is good for thinking. Want a cup?"

I did, and Charley Powell, a man with a lot on his mind, went for coffee. Shay arrived for work when he was gone, but when I got up to talk to her, she shook her head no.

"I don't feel like talking just yet. Give me a while and I'll be okay," she said.

Powell came back, gave me my coffee without a word, and returned to his nervous doodling.

"A wrong move can cost me my career. You're a free-lance. You move on."

"Yes," I said.

"But what if it's true? What if Wes was a Harry?"

I shrugged. "A lot of people'll say no big deal."

That riled him a trifle. "I'm not a lot of people, and neither are the people who bust their ass trying to write and edit a decent newspaper."

"Do I get my man?"

"You've got him." Powell got up and strolled to the far side of the city room, where he tapped a reporter on the shoulder. The reporter wore a tweed jacket with a collar twenty years out of date. He was in his early forties and had lost all the hair on the front of his head. He looked weary and distracted. I had an idea he thought he was being summoned to interview a malcontent to get him off Powell's back.

"John Denson, Bob Sander."

We shook hands.

"That's Bob spelled backwards," said Sander. He waited for Powell to tell him what to do next. Sander had accepted his fate. He wasn't going to be made an editor, but he was a professional. He did what was expected of him, did it well, and let other people worry.

"Have you told him what we want him to do?" I asked like Sander wasn't even there.

It didn't seem to bother him. "I can do a hell of an obit. I'm not bad at Kiwanis speeches. And give me a kid who chokes on a pear and I'll make 'em laugh or cry, take your pick," Sander smirked.

"As you can see, a real gem," said Powell.

"I like his style," I said.

"I once slipped a 'shit' past the desk in California," said Sander. He was warming to the task.

Powell shook his head.

I grinned.

Sander was rolling. "I did a feature on ladies' toenails that was picked by the wire services. I rode a bus all the way to Georgia and didn't come up with one single observation on man's inhumanity to man. I was proud of that one."

"Okay, okay . . ."

Sander interrupted. "I'm good at *non sequiturs,* too."

Powell told him about Wes Haggart and the Harry suspicion.

49

Sander shrugged his shoulders. "Does a bear shit in the woods? I once knew of a city councilman in Fresno who buggered goats. Everybody knew he did it but nobody cared. It was said he played a hell of a game of pinochle. Never could play cards myself. Struck me as a waste of time."

Bob Sander was a beaut.

Even Powell was curious.

"Was he a Republican or a Democrat?" Powell asked.

Sander thought about that a moment, furrowing his eyebrows as though the labor of thinking was almost too much for him. "Can't remember. Doesn't make any difference though, they're all the same. Goats or voters, what difference does it make? Nobody cares. Only thing that matters is food in your gut and a lay now and then."

"You could wind up breaking the law," Powell said.

Sander recoiled. "Will I get caught?"

"Shouldn't," I said. "But you can never tell."

"I could always write one of those asshole 'I was on the inside' stories and get people all worked up over the plight of crooks. It was blacks three weeks ago, women last week, queers this week. Crooks are due."

Powell couldn't help it. He grinned in spite of himself.

Sander had an audience and wasn't going to stop. "Do you know I walked in a parade with my daughter on my shoulders when Martin Luther King Jr. was murdered." He shook his head. "I was young then. After I was divorced I learned all the feminist lingo, figured it would get me some. Nothing. They all want Rhett Butler but won't admit it. I'll pass on the fags. Crooks I'm not sure about. Maybe I could sit in jail and watch 'Masterpiece Theatre' with an embezzler or something. The British let you see tits."

"Will you do it?" I asked.

"If Charley'll appear as a character witness at my trial?"

Powell was beginning to feel sorry he'd picked Sander. "Oh, hell yes," he said.

Powell had had enough of Sander. "You'll take him, then?"

"Why not?"

Sander grinned.

"Jesus Christ," Powell said disgustedly.

Sander, pleased with the screwball way he'd handled his audition, drifted back to his desk.

Powell watched him go and shook his head. "He may be a bit flaky, Denson, but he's smart, or I wouldn't have recommended him."

"I like his line about goats and voters. Right now I've got to go through Wes Haggart's notebooks before the cops get the idea. They'll be going through his apartment for physical evidence this morning and probably won't be around until this afternoon. I'll need a copyboy to Xerox the notebooks as I finish them."

"You mean 'copyperson.'"

"Huh?"

"We have to call them 'copypersons' these days, Guild insists on it. George Orwell would have puked."

"Yes, I'll need a copyperson to Xerox the notebooks as I go through them."

"No problem. And I think you're in luck. Haggart stored old notebooks in his desk."

Haggart took notes in a five-by-seven stenographer's notebook bound at the top with a wire spiral. He had mashed the spiral on the edge of his desk so he could store a pencil there and save wear and tear on his jacket pockets. He had dated each notebook on the first and last page so if some jerk challenged him in a libel suit, he could go directly to the right notebook. He had one year's worth stored in the one deep drawer of his desk. That was a bit of luck. Most reporters keep them only six months, if that long.

I opened what was the second most recent of his notebooks. The most recent would be in his apartment and in the hands of the cops by now. Haggart wrote with an abbreviated scrawl that was next to impossible to read. It took a while but I got the hang of his system. He left out articles, most vowels, and punctuation. Those he could add later. Direct quotes were preceded by a dash. He included only the most critical questions so he could be accurate when he wrote the story. He noted only facts, statistics, and quotes. There were no hunches,

51

guesses, or reminders to himself: he apparently kept those in his head. A single line drawn across the page separated one interview from the next.

The copyperson, a cheery teenage girl with braces on her teeth, brought me another cup of coffee. I settled down to work.

I struck a mother lode with the first turn of soil.

For some reason not made clear in the notes, Haggart had become interested in a squabble over salmon-fishing rights on the Tukionda River. The Tukionda was a salmon-rich stream on the southwest coast of Washington. At issue was whether the remnants of the Kiwika Indian tribe should have exclusive fishing rights on the Tukionda. The Indians said they did, the rights having been granted them in a treaty signed with the federal government in 1883. The government said they didn't in view of the fact that the dwindling tribe had disbanded as a legal entity in 1955.

The situation was clouded by the fact that few Kiwikas remained in the area and only three Indians, two brothers, Reuben and Samuel Slackwater, and Reuben's wife, Ethel, actually fished the river. The Slackwaters had for several years attempted to gillnet every fish that entered the Tukionda, a practice the Washington State Wildlife Commission argued would destroy the salmon run. No matter, the Slackwaters became a celebrated cause. Famous Hollywood actors and professional radicals on lecture tours demonstrated on their behalf.

The three Slackwaters declared that they constituted a tribe, but a federal judge, in a stunning moment of rationality, said no. Shortly thereafter, a panel of judges declared that at least 1,500 bona fide Kiwikas were needed to reincorporate the tribe. There were just 600 when they had called it quits.

The Slackwaters thereupon retained the Los Angeles detective agency of Chandler, Armstrong, and Hobbes to trace the scattered descendants of the Kiwikas. This latter fact had been dug up by Haggart. The Slackwaters, seasoned holders of press conferences, had been staying inside their tepees or wherever for several months. Haggart had a quote from the head of a large Seattle agency that a search of that nature would run about $500,000.

Where in hell would the Slackwaters get that kind of money? Haggart had also wondered and had pursued the matter.

The Slackwaters then hired Morris Weintraub, the most expensive lawyer in Seattle, to argue their case. Haggart had a "$100,000?" noted after that fact. He found that Weintraub had defended violations by Japanese fishing vessels that had been pushed farther from the coast by extended American claims of offshore fishing rights.

The vessels were run by an outfit named Kamada Ltd.

Kamada Ltd. was a subsidiary of Matsumura Industries, a Japanese multinational corporation.

When I got that far, I was reading Haggart's mind.

He had gone immediately to the library at the University of Washington to find out about Matsumura Industries. Matsumura had been put on the rack in a definitive article in the *Asian Economic Review,* a new magazine that attempted to tell all.

Haggart had just noted the highlights. That was enough.

Matsumura made motorcycles, television sets, precision instruments, computer parts, and sophisticated equipment for steel mills. Those items were just at the top of the list of their legitimate operations. The article suggested any manner of marginal and outright illegal activities. For example, Matsumura was heavily involved in pinball machines in Japan and through connections with the Yakuza, or Japanese mafia, allegedly controlled display space highly prized by book and magazine publishers.

After that Haggart had gone to interview the man himself, the famous Mr. Weintraub. He knew he had to be careful and so went to a Q. and A. system in his notebook.

Just before the Q. and A., Haggart had noted a lovely bit of information. The wholesale price of fresh salmon in the United States runs about $2.50 a pound. That same salmon, a delicacy in Japan, can bring as high as $12.50 a pound in Tokyo.

It was here that Charley Powell interrupted my work.

"John Anders is on the telephone. He says it's urgent that he talk to you." Powell had punched the hold button so Anders couldn't hear him.

"Tell him you scoured the city room for me and that I've vanished. You don't know where I am."

"Gotcha."

I returned to the Weintraub interview:

Q. Mr. Weintraub, how much is your fee for arguing the Slackwater case in the courts?

A. (long pause) That's privileged information between an attorney and his client.

Q. What is the relationship between the Slackwaters and the firm of Kamada Ltd.?

A. I don't know that firm.

Q. Are you certain?

A. Absolutely. And that's the end of this interview.

Morris Weintraub had lied through his teeth on the last question.

If Wes Haggart was a Harry and was trying to blackmail Matsumura Industries, he had nerve. I didn't think there was any question that Matsumura would be willing to murder three people to protect a $500,000 investment.

The Slackwater and Matsumura interviews and information were contained in two of Haggart's notebooks. I slid under his typewriter and wrote a story based on his notes. The lead was fairly straightforward. I hyped the story all I could without libeling the Slackwaters:

A Japanese multinational corporation with a subsidiary involved in offshore salmon fishing in the Pacific Northwest may be the financial angel behind a Kiwika Indian effort to gain legal rights to unlimited gillnetting in the Tukionda River.

I played it from there. Nice little story. The *Star* had computers programmed to scan copy written on a special IBM typewriter. I ended the story with the traditional "30," signifying that the story was finished. The end. The computer had been programmed to pick up on that, too. I took it to Charley Powell. "Who makes the decisions about what goes on page one, Charley?"

Charley frowned. "Max." It was a simple enough name.

But I knew from the way Charley said it that Max was someone different.

"Max?"

"Uh-huh. That's Max." Charley motioned with his head. Max was a hulking, ruddy-faced man in his late fifties. Despite having gone a bit to seed, he had an extraordinary presence. He was handsome, virile, and sported a Clark Gable mustache. He sat scowling over his desk. "His name is Max. He has a last name which nobody here can pronounce. It's maybe Polish, maybe Czech, maybe Serbo-Croatian, nobody knows for sure. He's just Max. Max is the news editor, Denson; he picks the page-one stories." Charley smirked.

"And?"

"And Max doesn't take shit from anybody. He hates greed, excess, bullshit, and the Establishment in almost all its forms. If he had his way, almost all politicians would be drawn and quartered in a public square."

I looked at Max, who had apparently heard his name mentioned and looked vaguely in our direction. Max's eyes narrowed. "How did he ever get to be news editor?"

Charley shook his head. "That's a good question, Denson. Men with his intelligence and imagination usually get screwed before they reach a position of power. You watch people like him. But Max made it somehow. He persevered. Max is a rare bird; he has a conscience. He bullies management; management bullies him. He loses in the end, but he makes them sweat."

"Do you think you could con him into pulling a clinker and replacing it with this?" I gave him the story I had written with Wes Haggart's by-line up top. I waited while Powell read the story.

"The Slackwaters are gonna have to trade their gill nets in for spinning rods after this one."

"I don't want you or Max to tell Anders."

Powell raised his eyebrows. "Why not?"

"Because editors put the interests of the corporation first. You and I will put a man's honor and the interests of our reader first, which is why they run the show and people like your friend Jenkins keep a bottle of whiskey in their desk."

55

"You don't have to worry about Max." Powell took my empty Styrofoam cup and returned it with three fingers of Hill & Hill. "Let me see." He went to Max's desk and squatted beside it. Max listened to Charley's story, blinked once, and looked at me. Charley returned to the city desk.

"Well?" I asked.

"Max says the world is off its feed today, no volcanos, no terrorist attacks, no government agency abusing the public, no politicians on the take."

"It's a slow news day?"

Charley grinned. "Exactly. But Max likes the story anyway. Says the Japanese think they can buy any damned thing they want."

"They're efficient."

"Do you think Matsumura had Wes killed?"

"They had reason. I think this story will eliminate any motive for doing some other poor bastard in."

"Like John Denson, for instance."

"Like John Denson," I said.

"It'll be on page one."

"You can box a note saying it was the last story Haggart turned in before he was murdered."

Powell nodded. "Not a bad touch. Done."

"Thanks," I said.

Powell paused. "Denson, I'm glad it's you with Shay and not some other jerk. She's an awful nice little gal, carries her heart right up front."

"I'll be careful," I said.

"Thank you, and do me a favor by not repeating this."

"No way. I'm going to take these two notebooks with me. When the copyperson finishes Xeroxing the rest, you stash them away somewhere safe for me, will you?"

"No problem."

6

I SAID GOOD-BYE to Shay, who was interviewing a man who had strolled into the city room claiming to have invented a foolproof way to run an automobile on household garbage. He was a tweedy-looking young man with a bony face and an intense, serious look about his eyes. Shay was politely asking him questions as though he were important and mattered. His views would be reported to the readers of the next edition; there would be a picture of him looking serious and intense. He never would be heard from again.

I once interviewed a man who had strolled into the city room looking and sounding like Humphrey Bogart. He announced he was running for governor. He said sports fans should vote for him because he was a wingback for the 1941 New York Giants. He said patrons of the arts should vote for him because he had once danced in a movie with Fred Astaire. He said he was Bogart's cousin. I figured there were worse reasons to vote for someone. So what if none of his claims checked out? What did it matter? I wrote the story and it turned out he was an escapee from a mental institution. People wrote letters to the editor claiming I was cruel.

I bet he still has the clipping.

I left Shay with her interview and escaped the *Star* building. I headed downtown and slipped into the first sleepy-looking bar I could find. It was empty except for the bartender and a man in his mid thirties who was drinking a whiskey and water and staring at nothing.

I took a stool two down from the whiskey drinker and ordered a draft beer. "Say," I said to the whiskey drinker.

He turned my way. "Yeah?"

"How would you like to make twenty bucks for a simple phone call? Nothing illegal, but I need some information."

He looked wary. "What makes you ask me?"

"Why not you? You're sitting here not doing anything." I tried a little beer.

The whiskey drinker shrugged. "Tell me what I have to do and then I'll tell you."

"Fair enough. I'll give you a number. A secretary will answer. You ask for Mr. Balkin. Tell her your name is Eric Hess and you deal in securities. When Balkin answers, identify yourself again and say you have a client interested in buying his Fielding Enterprises stock. Ask him if he's willing to sell. If he says yes, tell him you'll be getting back to him soon. Whether he says yes or no, ask him if there are any other members on the Fielding board of directors who would be willing to sell. Got that?"

"Can you write that out on a piece of paper so I won't screw up?"

I ripped a page out of my reporter's notebook. "No problem." I wrote out the chore, numbering each step, and gave him the twenty.

The whiskey drinker paused before he made the call. "Why don't you call him yourself?"

"He knows who I am. If I ask, the price will go up. You know how it is."

"Sure would be nice to know how it is," he said, and made the call. I picked the right man. He really was very good and made the appropriate "uh-huhs" and "I sees." He knew he'd suckered Balkin. When he hung up he grinned broadly. "He said he's not interested in selling his shares but I might see

58

Stuart Simpson, who is also on the board. He said it was a bull market for Fielding, as I should know. But he said Simpson had been badly hurt by a Canadian decision not to build a pipeline to a natural gas field where he is in up to his ass. Said Simpson needs the money."

I'd guessed right. Harold Balkin was on the board of directors of Fielding Enterprises. "You did well," I said. "How about buying me a beer?"

"Buy the man a beer," the whiskey drinker said. He waved expansively to the bartender. "Said if the government could just be talked into helping the Canadians, Simpson would be swimming in it. I'm here same time every day drinking and thinking. If you need any more phone calls, just drop around."

I made two phone calls, the first to Shay to tell her I would meet her at seven o'clock at the More. The second was to John Anders. He had lost much of the serene confidence he had had on the *Papa's Ark.*

"Christ, Denson, I've been looking all over hell for you. Where've you been?"

"You people thought you had a Harry on your hands and hired me to find out for sure. Where I've been is trying to do a job."

He groaned on the other end. "Like I said, where have you been, in Poughkeepsie? Wes Haggart is dead."

The trick here was for me to be calm and to not rile him too much. "He still could have been a Harry, Mr. Anders. The Seattle police department is conducting a murder investigation. The very first thing they'll do is look for a motive. A dead Harry will deliver the *Seattle Star* to Tobias Lane every bit as much as a live one. I assumed . . ."

Anders cut me short. "Don't assume anything. I want you off the scent until we can get together with Harold Balkin."

"Well, it's your newspaper."

"You're damned right it is!" he snapped back.

"Can you and Balkin get together for a meeting this afternoon?"

"When and where?"

"There's an awful plastic pancake house called The Gazebo two freeway exits past the U district. No local in his right mind

59

would go there to eat, only travelers. What do you say we meet at five o'clock and talk it over?"

Anders thought about that. "Okay, but if we don't show, don't be sore. I can't guarantee I can swing it."

"No big deal," I said.

Anders was able to swing it. I thought he might. They came gliding into The Gazebo's parking lot in Balkin's Mercedes Benz at a quarter past five. Balkin owned a Mercedes and a Porsche. They were both wearing double-knit golfing togs with white shoes. Anders looked especially ridiculous considering his short stature and bulk. He looked concerned.

The two of them joined me in a booth that featured pastel-colored plastic seats and a Formica tabletop. Balkin looked about with an uncertain curiosity, like he was visiting a prison lunchroom. He turned suddenly and grinned:

"What do you say we eat?"

"You buying?" I asked.

"Of course, why not?" he said cheerfully. Harold Balkin was slumming.

Anders had come up in the world and would just as soon have forgotten places like The Gazebo, but Balkin was the publisher, so Anders ordered with good grace if not relish. I ordered the most expensive steak in the house and a Jack Daniels on the rocks to whet my appetite.

When the drinks came, Balkin got quickly to the point:

"Now then, Mr. Denson, what is the situation as you see it, given, that is, the unusual reversal in Wes Haggart's good fortunes?"

Well, reversal is one way you could put it. "I can't see that anything has changed."

"Except that Wes Haggart's dead," said Anders.

"Like I told you earlier, Mr. Anders, Haggart could still have been a Harry, and if Hofstadter finds out during the murder investigation, he'll still sock it to you. Lane would still wind up with the newspaper."

"Then what good could you be?" asked Anders.

Anders obviously wanted to forget the whole thing. I wasn't sure about Balkin. "I could give you valuable warning so you could make the best out of a bad situation. There's that. Also

I should think you would want to know whether or not Wes Haggart was crooked." I figured what the hell, if I was going to get the hook, I could at least get the satisfaction of watching them squirm a bit.

Balkin regarded me mildly over his drink. "I just don't know," he said.

If I wasn't charming, I was still stupid. I pressed my disadvantage. "What I can't figure out, Mr. Balkin, is why you didn't tell your friend here you were the source of the Harry tip?"

Anders closed his eyes and kept them that way for a brief moment.

"By God, that was your man on the phone this afternoon. I wondered about that after I hung up!" Balkin looked at me with renewed interest. "They were right about you."

I shrugged. "I asked myself, why would anyone from Fielding Enterprises confess that an executive of one of their companies was suspected of arson? Friendship rarely extends that far. But suppose you had two investments to protect, one at Fielding and a second at the *Seattle Star*. It might be possible to protect both flanks with one stroke—me."

"Precisely," said Balkin. He didn't seem especially chagrined at having been found out.

I relaxed a bit and had some more Jack Daniels. Balkin could veto Anders. He was charming, but cold-blooded where his wallet was at stake. I had one chance, a long one, of pursuing the question of whether Wes Haggart was a Harry. I wanted to know the answer.

"There's also the question of why Leslie Dunham was rummaging through Mr. Anders's desk for Haggart."

Anders damned near tipped his drink over.

I looked surprised and not a little bewildered. "Didn't you tell Mr. Balkin?"

"Oh?" said Balkin.

I told them the story of Samantha Becker.

I met Anders's eyes and he maintained control admirably. He was determined to keep his mouth shut until Balkin had spoken.

"What do you think?" asked Balkin. He sensed Anders's

61

discomfort, and his urbane coolness was not a little sadistic.

I swirled the ice in my drink. "I think there are two possibilities. One is that Haggart was a Harry and was using Leslie to give him warning in case anything went wrong. For the second possibility you have to understand what made Haggart tick. The greatest coup that Haggart could pull would be to pin something on his own editor in chief . . ."

"Now wait just one damned minute." Anders leaned across the booth.

"I'm not saying you've done anything dishonest. What I am saying is that Haggart may have been fishing for an angle. After all, no one but Leslie knew what he was up to. Leslie was in love with him. And if he didn't find anything worthwhile, who was the wiser? But when he found out you people were going to rendezvous on a fishing boat with a private detective, he smelled a real story. I must say he got a little cute with the Samantha business."

Anders relaxed noticeably. "I agree with Harold. They were right about you. Which still leaves the question of who killed the son of a bitch?"

"A gentleman hired by Matsumura Industries," I said. I wasn't sure about that at all, but I had to buy time. I told them the story of the Slackwaters and Morris Weintraub. I didn't tell them the story would be in the next edition of their newspaper.

They sat there, wide-eyed, the editor and publisher of the *Seattle Star*.

"So he was a Harry," said Anders.

"I don't know. I'm not trying to be cute, but I just don't know. I can't know until I've eliminated all the possibilities. That's why I want you two to keep me on the job. What you're paying me is peanuts in the long run. I just may save you a bloody fortune in grief and newspaper subscriptions in the short run." I waited.

"Done," said Balkin. "Stay on it."

The Publisher Speaketh. Thy Will Be Done.

"Good idea," said Anders.

It was pretty how Anders tumbled. First the one who counted, then the other.

62

7

WE FINISHED OUR MEAL, which wasn't all that bad, and I followed Balkin's big Mercedes out of The Gazebo's parking lot. We had no sooner swung onto the freeway entrance ramp than it really began to rain. The rain lashed and flayed the city. I slowed the Fiat to a crawl and soon lost the Mercedes's tail-lights in the confusion. I took the next exit off the freeway and stopped at a Safeway to buy a head of cauliflower. I wanted the cauliflower for drinking beer with Shay at the More. When I came out, the rain was still coming and the parking lot was an enormous lake.

When I stepped into the More, soaking wet and head of cauliflower in hand, I was met with what can only be described as a bizarre scene. Virtually the entire city room was in the More, together with sportswriters, cartoonists, editorial writers, and the women from the feature section. It was absolutely standing room only. The harried waitresses set pitchers of beer on the counter so the assembled staff of the *Star* could help itself. The room was blue with cigarette smoke. I searched the mob for Shay and finally spotted her waving frantically for me to join her. She must have arrived early, because she had a seat in a booth.

I started breaking flowerets off my head of cauliflower on my way through the bodies.

"I thought you'd never get here," she shouted above the din. She gave me her seat in the booth, hopped up on my lap, and leaned close to my ear. "Where have you been?" she asked.

We switched ears. "Trying to find out who murdered Wes Haggart. What's going on here?"

We switched again. "Everybody on the staff put ten bucks in a pot. The money pays for the beer tonight. Anything left over will go for flowers on the three graves tomorrow. Powell's coming over."

"Hmmmm." I shrugged. I started munching cauliflower.

She joggled me with her shoulder. It was clear I didn't completely understand the significance of Powell's coming over. "As far as anyone knows, Powell's never been over here in his life," she all but shouted in my ear. "Powell's drunk. He never drinks. He eats all his meals by himself out of a paper bag in the city room. He said he wanted to give a eulogy for Wes Haggart tonight. Said it was his duty as city editor."

Shay had no sooner said that than the crowd suddenly quieted. I knew without seeing him enter that Charley Powell had arrived at the watering hole of his reporters to comment on the life of Wes Haggart. It was a moment that would be storied. Nobody wanted to miss it.

There was a momentary confusion, and the venerable city editor stepped from the crowd wearing baggy wool trousers and a rumpled corduroy jacket. He looked hollow-eyed and haggard. Shay was right: he was drunk. He looked around at the faces he worked with every day, swayed slightly but with an odd dignity, and was gripped by a racking cough. He recovered and spotted Shay and me in the booth; I thought momentarily that he was going to cry.

Others saw it too and hoped, as I did, that he could maintain control. He did. He leaned toward Shay and me.

"It's a terrible business," he said softly.

The black bags under Charley Powell's eyes glistened with moisture. He swabbed them dry with the back of his corduroy jacket, which was nearly threadbare at the elbows. He straightened himself to his full height, which was considerable, and addressed the room in a voice that was surprisingly clear.

"We're here tonight to honor Wes Haggart in a way he would have wanted and in a manner appropriate to newspapermen." Straight to the point. Powell paused and swallowed. "We're here for the unadorned facts, simply and concisely put. Rhetoric has no place here. We try not to inflict it on our readers; there is no reason why we should endure it ourselves. How many here can honestly say he was Wes Haggart's friend?"

It was an awful question. Powell waited for an answer. The room was quiet except for breathing and swallowing. A woman wept softly.

"Let's be honest: not many, would you say? We admired his reporting skills, but with the exception of Leslie Dunham, who possibly died because of it, I doubt if any of us really liked him, much less loved him. I knew him as well as most just from editing his copy. I can tell you, for example, that he was incapable of writing a story that would make anyone laugh or cry. He knew power and how it worked. He knew about greed and avarice. He knew the dark side of public men. He brought mayors and governors down a notch or two. I can remember, you can too, how he grinned when he reread his exposés over a cup of coffee. Does anybody have a spare mug of beer?"

The newspaper's editorial cartoonist, a large man who affected a western appearance with cowboy hats and sheepskin vests, handed him a mug. As Wes Haggart had insisted on the unvarnished truth about others, he was himself being subjected to that terrible standard. I could feel Shay breathing as she leaned back against me.

Charley Powell drained half the mug in one pull, held it out to be refilled, then continued:

"We deal every day with people who have an ax to grind. Most people try to use us. Almost all of them lie just a little. We see daily the sham of noble causes. We see good and well-intentioned men crushed. We see the inexorable rise of mean-spirited liars and demagogues. We cover public hearings on decisions we know have already been made. We report as news events staged by public relations men. We write impassioned editorials about Mexican politics and ignore corruption in our backyard. We refuse to write honestly and directly about the problems of blacks for fear of being labeled racists. We refuse, for fear of being branded illiberal, to address the plunder of the public treasury. We go easy on the excesses of business for fear of our editors and publishers. All of that you know well." Powell paused to clear his throat and have some more beer. He looked at Shay and me over the rim of his mug.

"The recourse is cynicism. We retreat from conviction. We identify with no one or no thing. The weakest of us succumb entirely and become devoid of feeling and compassion, which is what makes us human and civilized. That happened to Wes Haggart. So he set out in his cold and brutal manner to have his revenge. As a result, he became an honored reporter, a prize-winning newspaperman. People said yes, that's what newspapers should be doing: let the bastards have it. As his reputation grew, so did that of the *Star*; we all shared in his glory. I did as his city editor. You did as his colleagues. His reputation did not come without cost. Most of you are divorced; some of you are alcoholics. You know about those costs." Here Charley Powell paused for his kicker:

"No matter what happens, I think that's what we should remember. He was the best of us and the worst of us."

Charley Powell's eulogy was clear and to the point, the way he liked newspaper copy. He was finished.

What he said was true: Wes Haggart was one hell of a reporter but a miserable son of a bitch as a human being.

The noise resumed. It was a shade livelier than it had been before Charley Powell made his appearance. The reason, perhaps, was that the employees of the *Star* no longer felt obliged to lie about Wes Haggart.

Powell came over and squatted in front of Shay and me. He wavered momentarily and almost lost his balance. "I told you I wanted you to find out who killed him, Denson. I also want you to finish whatever it was he was working on when he was killed. I don't think he was killed because of the Matsumura business."

"I don't either," I said.

We watched Charley Powell disappear through the smoke

and people. Nobody congratulated him on his eulogy of Wes Haggart.

"I don't think Matsumura had anything to do with it either," Shay said when he left.

"A regular sleuth," I said. Charley Powell wasn't dumb. Shay wasn't either.

"For some reason I don't feel like hanging around the More," she said.

"I've got some pastrami. Good stuff. We could drink screw top and watch the city lights from my place."

"Ahh," said Shay. "Sounds good; we can pick up a six-pack on the way."

"We'll drink to Wes. May he not have been a Harry."

"We'll drink to Wes."

8

WE GATHERED AT A cemetery the next morning to bury Wes Haggart. It was cloudy but not raining when we assembled on the wet grass. It had apparently been Haggart's wish not to have a church service. His body was in a gray metal casket beside a hole in the ground. It was protected by a green canvas awning. His mother and sister had intervened, so there was a minister at the burial, a Unitarian. He was a hollow-eyed young man with a wispy beard.

The young minister, who was wearing dark glasses, looked pious enough as we gathered around the hole. There was general snuffling and blowing of noses. A siren wailed faintly and poignantly in the distance. Haggart's mother, a plump woman with graying, thin hair, watched the minister with some anxiety. So did his sister, who was not yet plump but one day would be. She was there with her two small sons, both awkward in white shirts, and her husband, a tall man who adjusted his glasses and stared at his feet. Their fears were justified.

The minister opened a book, which we could all see was a college anthology of English literature, and began reading poetry by William Blake. It didn't make any sense to any of us, although Haggart's mother was moved to tears. His sister looked like she could kick the minister in the shins. If she had, we would have encouraged her not to stop.

We rode back to the newspaper in silence.

Shay and I walked into the city room with Powell.

"Ring Lardner or somebody would have been okay," Powell said.

The city room went back to work. Wes Haggart was dead. Nobody would miss him especially. His stories always had a touch of the self-righteous People's Prosecutor that was wearying to anybody old enough to know genuine white hats and black hats are hard to come by. But there was an unspoken fear that knocking off hard-ass reporters might somehow become fashionable, like ex-cons who return to haunt prosecuting attorneys and judges. It is for the same reason cops turn on cop killers with a vengeance.

Why the slender Japanese who represented Matsumura Industries chose to turn so vehemently on Charley Powell was not so obvious. He was a slender, elegant man dressed in a dark blue suit and white shirt. He was accompanied by a hulking Caucasian who glanced nervously at the city room and managed somehow to look embarrassed. There was no doubt in anybody's mind that this visit was the result of the salmon-fishing story. If an American corporation gets burned by a story, its executives shut up and wait till the editors get tired of the story. A good reporter will take the smallest scrap of information and ride it for all it's worth. But this man, a Japanese, had a different way of looking at the press.

"I would like to speak to the editor in charge of the salmon-fishing story in yesterday's paper," said the Japanese.

Charley Powell looked up from his desk, affecting a wide-eyed, simple innocence. He had handled thousands of complainers in his time. He was a professional with complainers. He handled a complainer the way Mickey Mantle used to handle a curve ball that hung over the heart of the plate. "I'm glad you liked our story. We work very hard to serve our readers." He looked the Japanese square in the eye.

"My name is Hashimoto Masuo; I'm the general manager of

69

Matsumura operations here in Seattle. I can assure you I'm not here to offer you congratulations."

"Charley Powell." Charley rose to shake his hand.

"We may have grounds for action," the Caucasian put in.

"This is our counsel, Mr. Dennis Johnson," said Hashimoto.

Powell looked like he was having a painful bowel movement. "Oh, bullshit! You want to go to court and prove we fucked up a fact, go ahead. If you can prove it now, we'll run a retraction in our next edition."

Hashimotosan looked embarrassed on Powell's behalf. "I'm sure nobody will be going to court, Mr. Powell. I'm sure everything will be worked out if we just work together."

The use of the pronoun "we" and the suggestion that any jerk could casually stroll into a newsroom and threaten a city editor enraged Charley Powell. "What do you mean 'we'; are you pregnant or do you have a turd in your pocket?"

Hashimoto's eyes looked glazed. "This is not a civilized way of doing business," he said softly. Caps on his teeth made it look like he had a mouth of solid gold when he spoke. "We had an agreement. I'm surprised at you. I was under the impression that you were honorable men here at the *Star*."

Charley Powell suddenly looked interested. The mere suggestion to Charley that one of his reporters had made an agreement not to publish information was outrageous. He was thinking, I knew, of Wes Haggart. He looked my way. I encouraged him to continue with a two-handed pushing gesture. "I apologize, Mr. Hashimoto, I'm not sure I know what agreement you're talking about. If you could be more specific."

Hashimoto glared at him. "The agreement, as you know, was among gentlemen."

Powell tried to look accommodating. "As I said, Mr. Hashimoto, I don't know what agreement you're talking about. If you could be more specific."

Hashimotosan glared at him. "The agreement, as you know, was among gentlemen."

Powell's temper was ready to blow, but he was restraining himself so I could hear the exchange. "There is no question of an agreement, Mr. Hashimoto. The only agreement this paper has is an oddly moral one to give the reader the facts as much as possible. The question is whether or not Mr. Haggart's article was true. If it contained statements that are not true, that's another matter; we'll retract anything we reported that is not true."

Hashimoto blinked once, twice, at Charles Powell, barbarian. "That's not the issue at all, Mr. Powell. The issue is one of honor among gentlemen and the fact that you have destroyed a half-million-dollar investment by Matsumura Industries."

Powell wanted to tell Hashimoto he didn't give a damn about his half million. "I understand your concern, Mr. Hashimoto, but I have a newspaper to run."

The Caucasian shifted his weight from one foot to another. He understood what was happening but couldn't do anything about it.

"This would never have happened in Japan," said Hashimoto. "In Japan the press and the business community work together."

Powell could see the argument coming full circle. "I understand there are differences, Mr. Hashimoto."

What we were seeing was extraordinary. Hashimoto must have been livid with rage to confront Powell personally. The correct way would have been through a third party. The lawyer should have been doing the talking.

"Then perhaps you could do us a favor. We would like your paper to apologize to Matsumura and to run an article explaining to your readers the success we've had with our fisheries in Hokkaido. We would be happy to pay for the expenses of a reporter and photographer."

Powell closed his eyes, kept them closed for a moment, then looked at Hashimoto straight on. "We never apologize for reporting the truth, Mr. Hashimoto. I believe I said that already."

Hashimoto took that calmly. "Is it because we are Japanese, perhaps?"

"It would be the same if your name were Bernard Schwartz or One Hung Low."

The Caucasian repressed a smirk with effort. Hashimoto didn't get the joke. "Your Mr. Haggart was a persistent and obstinate man."

"He was a good reporter," said Powell.

"He was no gentleman," said Hashimoto. He turned and strolled from the room, followed by the big lawyer, who turned and gave a helpless gesture with his hands.

When Hashimoto was gone, Powell motioned for me to come to his desk. "That charming little fellow responsible for Wes Haggart's murder?"

I looked in the direction Hashimoto had gone. "I don't know. I don't think so. But I'll tell you one thing: I'll make book he has an M.B.A. from Harvard."

Powell furrowed his brow. "How do you figure that?"

"Could be the University of Wisconsin. No Japanese businessman would come on like that in a city room of a newspaper in Nippon. No sir. His English is Japanese. His manners are American as hell."

"Maybe he had a Hungarian roommate," Powell said. "Hungarians are nuts."

"I think I'd better pursue this agreement business."

A quick check of the telephone directory told me that Matsumura Industries had a suite in one of Seattle's fanciest downtown office buildings. The building wasn't far from the *Star* so I took shank's mare. Good for the cardiovascular system.

There was a young woman in the elevator with me. We stared at one another as we were propelled to the upper levels of the building. We stared, saying nothing, for fourteen floors, when I got off. I regretted that I hadn't asked her to marry me or something equally outrageous just to see what she would do. Have me arrested, probably. The reception room at Matsumura Industries looked like a promotion for Japan Airlines. There was an enormous color photo of Mount Fuji in crisp, blue air. Since Fuji hadn't seen crisp, blue air for several decades, I wondered how they managed the picture. There were delicate geishas in kimonos with delicate prints and white makeup. And a large poster of the old Imperial Palace in Kyoto.

The girl at the desk, however, was a blonde with giant boobs. She had pale green goo above cornflower blue eyes. She looked up and blinked twice, knowing I was staring at her breasts. "Yes?" she asked.

I didn't tell her what was on my mind. "I would like to speak to Mr. Hashimoto, please. My name is John Denson and I'm a reporter with the *Seattle Star*. There was a misunderstanding with Mr. Hashimoto at our office earlier today which our editors regret."

"Oh?" She raised her eyebrows. "Will you have a seat, please? I'll only be a moment."

I sat and leafed through a *National Geographic* with a lead story on Japanese pearl divers. I thought there might be a story on Japanese terraces or the cargo cult of New Guinea, but nothing. I wasn't disappointed. The blonde was back.

"Mr. Hashimoto will see you now," she said.

I walked into the office where the impeccable Hashimotosan waited behind an impressive teak desk. He motioned for me to sit.

I sat.

"Mr. Denson, is it? How can I be of help?" Hashimoto bowed slightly but kept his eyes on me.

I bowed in return. "Our Mr. Powell is a hasty man. He often speaks too quickly and regrets it later. We in the Pacific Northwest have many ties with Japan, as you know, and neither Mr. Powell nor the other editors of the *Star* would like his intemperate remarks to harm our relations. He sends his apologies."

Hashimoto brightened perceptibly. "I am afraid there may have been a cultural problem."

"Yes, we think that also."

I was being sent as a face-saving third party. Hashimoto understood that completely.

"May we be of service then, Mr. Denson?"

"In our office this morning you mentioned an agreement. Mr. Powell is confused. He tells me he knows of no agreement between our paper and you, but if there is one, the *Star* stands by its word."

Hashimoto cleared his throat softly and adjusted a neat stack of papers on the teak desk. "The agreement was with your reporter, Mr. Haggart, but unfortunately he was murdered."

"With Mr. Haggart?"

"Yes," said Hashimoto. He waited.

"Well, I'm afraid there was a misunderstanding. He was apparently murdered before he told his editors of the agreement."

"Oh?"

"Yes. Another reporter wrote that story from notes that were found after his death."

"Oh!" Hashimoto realized he'd been screwed by circumstances. That he could understand. "Well then, I'm very sorry I accused your Mr. Powell of being dishonorable. Will you extend him my apologies?"

"Certainly." I went through my polite bowing routine. "So that we may know, Mr. Hashimoto, could you please tell us the arrangement you made with Mr. Haggart?"

He held up the palms of his hands. "I don't know what harm it would cause. Two days before Mr. Haggart was murdered, he called us and told us the result of his investigation. He said for ten thousand dollars he would not write the story."

"And you said?"

Hashimoto looked surprised. "We said, 'Of course!' We had an investment to protect, after all. It seemed to us a small matter, really. Agreements such as this are common enough in Asia."

"How was the contact made?"

Hashimoto didn't understand completely. He cocked his head.

I rephrased the question. "How did Mr. Haggart go about making his proposition?"

He understood that well enough. "By telephone."

"By telephone?"

Hashimoto looked surprised. "There's nothing unusual about that. We knew Mr. Haggart had been conducting an investigation. Our Indian friends told us as much. So did our lawyer. Frankly, we were concerned until he called and made his offer. We had been planning to contact him, but it was much better this way—he moved first."

I nodded my head in understanding. "Of course. Of course," I said. "Did Mr. Haggart say he had cleared the arrangement with his editors?"

Hashimoto smiled. "He said part of the money would go to your Mr. Powell."

"Charles Powell?" I was beginning to sweat and could smell myself.

"Yes, that's the man, the same one I talked to earlier. That's why I was surprised that he was ignorant of our agreement." I gave him a look that said I understood his problem and agreed he'd been screwed. "You have to understand, Mr. Hashimoto, that Mr. Haggart was operating entirely on his own and said nothing at all to Mr. Powell."

Hashimoto looked at the ceiling. "I think I see that now, Mr. Denson. I thank you for coming. Do you think there is still a possibility of sending a reporter to Japan?" He leaned forward slightly.

"Under the circumstances, I'm sure the paper might consider it. I'm not sure what the decision would be." Not in ten thousand years, Jack, I thought to myself. I rose from my seat. "Thank you very much for your time, Mr. Hashimoto. I know your time is very valuable."

He rose, bowed slightly, and shook my hand. "Not at all, Mr. Denson, not at all. I'm very pleased that you came."

He showed me to the door.

9

THE FIRST THING I DID back at the *Star* was to get a cup of coffee and head for the newspaper library. A plump woman in her early forties asked what I would like.

"I want your complete file on John Anders. I want everything, every bundle."

"Mr. Anders?" she asked. She blinked once, twice, but didn't move from the counter.

"That's it," I said cheerily. I fiddled with my yellow pencil.

She hesitated. Librarians never ask reporters what they want clips for but this, in her mind, was clearly an unusual request. "Our Mr. Anders?"

I could have gone into some kind of tantrum, but I didn't. "When Wes Haggart died, the guys on nightside found out they really didn't know anything about him. Powell was enraged that Haggart's own paper garbled the facts of his life. He wants me to do an obit on John Anders and the other honchos in this outfit; if Anders gets squashed by a falling tree on deadline, we'll have everything ready to go."

"Oh, I see," she smiled.

"We do it for movie stars and politicians, why not do it for our own editor?"

"Ahhh," she said, and moved off to get my clips.

I spread the clips on my desk and set about to piece together the life of John Anders. I took notes on the good bits on my typewriter. When I was finished I rearranged them in chronological order with a pair of scissors and rubber cement. Most of the clips were about Anders accepting this or that award for the newspaper or telling the readers of the acquisition of a syndicated columnist who was the sage of the twentieth century or a comic strip that would have the reader guffawing each day. I had a lot of work to do; none of the clips really said much about Anders himself. It was all straightforward stuff:

Anders was fifty-nine years old. His wife had died of cancer when he was fifty-three, and he had two daughters, Beth, a graduate student at Cornell, and Amy, a senior at Georgetown University. He was born in Escondido, California, the son of a civil engineer. His father was killed in an automobile accident when he was sixteen, and his mother, a former Miss San Diego, remarried six months later. Anders was bright and, for reasons which were not clear in the clips, wanted to be a newspaperman from the beginning. He attended and was graduated from UCLA, where he was editor of the student newspaper his senior year. He spent the summers as a combination writer and photographer on a small-town daily in northern California. He remained interested in cameras, and in later years became an accomplished photographer with one-man shows in Seattle, Boston, and Denver. Following his graduation from UCLA, he spent six years in the San Francisco bureau of the Associated Press and three years in the Washington bureau of the *Los Angeles Times*.

At age thirty-one, Anders was appointed a Nieman Fellow and spent a year at Harvard University. While at Harvard, he met and married Anjanette LaChance, a Vassar student and the pretty daughter of Richard LaChance, editor of the *Boston Globe*. His father-in-law made him city editor of the *Globe,* where he remained for four years until he moved to Detroit, where both his daughters were born and where he served as managing editor of the *Detroit Free Press* for seven years.

At age forty-two, he had the experience to become editor of his own paper. The owners of the *Seattle Star* agreed and gave him his chance.

From everything I could gather from the clips, he hadn't muffed it. The *Star* had grown in both circulation and reputation and had recently converted from letterpress to offset with extraordinary savings in back-shop labor costs.

I wrote an obit from my notes to satisfy the librarian and prevent gossip about what I was doing. I reread my notes to see if there was a smell about Anders. There wasn't.

It was then that I noticed Shay reading my notes upside down. I caught her eyes and she raised an eyebrow over her left blue.

"You're wondering what this has to do with Wes Haggart?"

She nodded yes and took a sip out of a cup of coffee.

"What if I told you the editor of this newspaper is a Harry?"

"A Harry?"

"After our friend Mr. Karafin of the *Philadelphia Inquirer* who went on the take about fifteen years back."

"John Anders?"

"The very same. The guy with the cigars."

Shay sat back in her chair and began twisting a strand of her blonde hair with a finger. "You've gotta be out of your mind."

I shook my head. "We have even better reason to think Wes Haggart may have been on the take before he was killed. That's why I was hired mysteriously when management was trying to cut back the staff."

Shay looked at Charley Powell, then back at me. Charley was bent over some copy, scowling. "Let me get this straight: you were put on the staff as a detective, not a reporter, and your job is to find out if the editor of this paper and Wes Haggart were both on the take?"

"That isn't quite it," I said. "It was one or the other." I told her about Leslie's rummaging of Anders's desk and Samantha's quizzing about my fishing trip. "We have to get this sorted out before it gets public and destroys the *Star*."

She looked at Charley Powell. "How on earth would it destroy the paper? Him, maybe, but not the *Star*."

I shook my head. "As one of Tobias Lane's sheets." I told her about Ruth Balkin Trotter's finances.

Shay closed her eyes.

"Charley said yesterday I could have you to help me out. It's voluntary only; you don't have to do it."

She flipped her blonde hair to one side with an angry twist of her neck. "Count me in. But I'll tell you right now I don't believe Wes was on the take—Anders either."

"I hope you're right. But let me talk to Charley for a minute, then we'll see if we can't figure a way to sort this mess out."

"I think you're wrong, John."

"You never know." I got up and went to see Charley Powell. I told him about my night with Samantha Becker. I told him about Harold Balkin and Fielding Enterprises. I told him about my meeting with Balkin and Anders at The Gazebo. "There are only two reasons why Haggart would go to the trouble and risk of having Leslie Powell rummage through Anders's desk: Wes was a Harry and was worried management was on to him, or Wes suspected Anders was a Harry and was trying to find out more."

Charley didn't say anything. He had several dozen press releases piled in a grand heap on his desk. He picked up one, read the logo on the corner, and flipped it back on the pile. "Look at this self-serving bullshit." With both hands he angrily swept the entire pile of releases into a wastepaper basket. "So now you gotta check out the editor of this newspaper in addition to our best reporter. Am I also to deduce from this that our editor may be a murderer as well?"

"It looks like that's a possibility that can't be overlooked. I'll have to check it out."

"And try to find out if Wes Haggart was on the take."

"Yes."

"There's also the question of the murderer."

"That too."

Powell shook his head. "Did Balkin specifically ask you to check Anders out?"

"No, but it has to be done."

"Yes," Charley Powell said. He knew it had to be done.

"You know, Denson, if Wes Haggart was a Harry, he's lucky I didn't get ahold of him before the killer did."

I'd considered that possibility but I hadn't said anything. Charley might have done his damndest to throttle Haggart, but he wouldn't murder two innocent young women in the process. "I'll let you know what I find."

I went to the john, and when I got back to my desk, Shay was interviewing a television producer from Los Angeles who was shooting a program about Bigfoot. He was a high roller, a dazzler with expensively sloppy clothes and a gold chain around his neck. He had two young things with him. They had large breasts on slender torsos and pants molded to their butts. The dazzler was bored with them, however, and was casing Shay. She was trying hard not to show she was flattered. The dazzler loved himself: this was Hollywood, baby, Big Time!

"This man the flack from Boeing?" I asked Shay.

The dazzler's left wrist dropped slightly but he recovered and regarded me mildly. "I'm from Los Angeles," he said.

I shrugged and rolled a piece of paper into my typewriter.

"Are you finished?" he demanded of Shay. He wasn't finished with impressing her.

"Sure, I've got enough," she said.

The dazzler glided from the room followed by the butts and large-breasted torsos.

I watched them until they disappeared through the door. "Sorry," I said to Shay.

"You know, John, I think he liked me."

Sander suddenly appeared. He had been eavesdropping. "Yeah, you, young boys, German shepherds, and knotholes in cedar fences."

"I think the three of us need to go somewhere and have a talk."

"The three of us?" Shay looked at Sander.

Sander leered. "A *ménage à trois,* my love. Denson's for it and me, I'm game for anything."

"Charley's detailed Sander here to help us out."

"Sander?"

Sander pretended to pick his nose. "Everything's possible in the modern world, my love."

"Well, group, shall we be off?" I led the way, brave John Denson. Sander tried to get an angle on the top of Shay's blouse on our way down the stairs. She caught him at it.

"Won't do any good, Bob, I'm wearing a bra. Don't have that much anyway."

Sander shrugged. "Only need a mouthful. That top button must not work, huh?"

Shay flipped it with her finger. "Never have tried it."

We chose a place called "In a Pig's Eye," which contained a few drunks of indeterminate middle-class status talking about the Seahawk's quarterback. It was not a place Sander or I would have picked, but Shay liked it. Sander seemed not at all rebuffed by Shay. I caught him trying the top of her blouse again, bra or no.

We settled in a booth with stuffed plastic seats and backs and ordered a large pitcher of dark. Sander stared absently into space. I didn't know where to begin.

"Well now, this is jolly," said Shay.

"We know Wes Haggart was interested in Anders's office. If we can find out why, I think we'll know whether Wes was a Harry or not and possibly why he was murdered. He was after an exposé or running scared, one or the other."

Shay looked blank. To her it was inconceivable that so elegant and refined a man as John Anders could be misusing his position. All things were possible to Wes Haggart. If you knew about maggots, you knew about gangrene. Haggart knew about maggots and was enraged.

Sander knew about maggots but didn't care. "Beats hell out of me, Red Ryder."

"Lust or money, what do you think?"

Shay said nothing.

Sander brightened. "That turd? Lust?"

I agreed and said so.

Sander wasn't finished. "Course maybe he hangs out down at the Y, groping young boys. That'd be juicy." He grinned sadistically. "We could have him write a first-person account in the Lifestyle section. You know, one of those 'I'm-not-a-pervert-this-is-just-an-alternate-preference' stories. It's all very normal, fondling young boys. The mayor would give him a special award for contributing to the understanding of minorities."

"You're disgusting," said Shay.

"You'll learn," Sander said, and gave her an obscene leer.

Sander didn't mean to be taken completely seriously and Shay understood that.

"Money is most likely," I said. "Anders is the only man in the newspaper with a hand in both directing the coverage of news and writing editorials for the opinion pages. One possibility, and it may be impossible to prove, is that he was using the newspaper to force the price of local stocks up or down. The first thing we do is find out where he has his money invested, then check that against the clips at the newspaper."

"How do you do that?" asked Shay.

"A little B and E."

"What's that?"

"You want to tell her, Bob?"

"Breaking and entering," Sander said. "I guess I'm supposed to trail along, passing gas and tripping over lamps?"

"That's about it," I said.

"You done this kind of thing before?"

"For Uncle Sam. Not since. Well, sort of not since."

"That's like being almost pregnant," Sander said.

Shay didn't say anything. She looked at me like I was a bit nuts.

"There's no other way."

"Listen, you two guys are like Slim Pickens and Woody Allen doing a Clint Eastwood caper. Three people were killed, and you're saying John Anders may have had a motive."

I shrugged. Sander giggled. "I'm not fast but I'm awkward," he said.

"Do you carry a pistol?" asked Shay.

It was a fair question. "I have a license for one in this state, in Oregon, and in California."

"But do you carry one?"

"Sam trained me to shoot at cardboard targets that popped up in front of me."

"That's not what I asked."

"When I was with Sam I was instructed to waste a man once and couldn't do it."

"So?" She was persistent, was Shay.

"So I don't carry a weapon. I can tap a phone and pick a lock. Those things Sander and I will be doing."

"What about me?"

"Not you."

Shay reddened. She was angry.

I looked straight on into her blues. "I'm no big loss. You are."

I meant it and she knew I meant it. She was touched. "What do I do while you two are going through your cat-burglar routine?"

"Nothing today, maybe a whole lot tomorrow. I'd suggest you give all your hard stuff to Charley for someone on general assignment."

"What can I do? I don't know judo and I can't shoot a gun."

"You pinned Sander here with a one-button takedown."

Shay backed off. "Oh, come on, John."

"Takes brains too, Shay. One without the other won't do."

"Sure," she said. "Listen, maybe I'll surprise you two."

Shay Harding was used to Bob Sander. She worked with him. His leering and his cynicism were partly an act. They were his idea of humor. They helped him survive; she knew that. Shay was a good reporter. She had proven herself in the city room with no less a city editor than Charley Powell.

She didn't like being underestimated.

She had given me warning, in her oblique way. It was my fault I didn't pay any attention.

10

WE LEARNED FROM POWELL that John Anders had gone to San Francisco to attend an Associated Press gathering for West Coast editors. It was a rainy night. It seems to rain every night in Seattle; there was no reason to wait. We had something to do that had to be done.

We left Shay listening to Bobby Darin sing "Mack the Knife" on the jukebox at the More and climbed into my Fiat. It was 2 A.M. and the streets were nearly empty. Sander tuned into a country and western station. We listened to songs about lost love and lonesome truckers.

"God that stuff's awful," Sander said. He made no move to change the station. "Just think, Anders won't run X-rated ads in the paper, but I'll bet he's down there in San Francisco rubbing his sixty-year-old paunch up against a nineteen-year-old whore."

My lights reflected off the wet pavement, so I could hardly see where I was going. Sander checked the map while I worked my way high into the hills of northwest Seattle. We made one slow pass by Anders's address. It was an ultramodern house that featured cubes, triangles at odd angles, skylights, glass to excess, lofts, and cathedral ceilings.

"Kid with a slingshot'd have a good time with that," said Sander.

I parked the Fiat on a side street. A house two doors down had all the lights on. We heard a man's voice. A woman giggled. The sounds of jazz on a stereo competed with the rain.

"That's Councilman Daw's place. Runs a regular whorehouse." Sander wiped some moisture from the window to watch the house. "Cops make sure everything's okay."

Councilman Arlo Daw was a notorious woman chaser and drunk. He also liked cops and saw to it that the Seattle Police Department was taken care of. The Seattle police took care of Councilman Daw.

"A good place to leave the Fiat. In neighborhoods like this, cops know which cars belong and which ones don't." I got out my black leather valise and produced rubber gloves for Sander and myself. I felt like Bogey.

"Makes me feel like George Raft," said Sander.

"I was thinking Bogart."

"Raft's better. I like those mean little eyes."

The rain obligingly relented for our quarter-mile walk back to Anders's house. It was a brisk night. Our breath came in puffs. The city lights were below us to our left. Seattle is gorgeous at night. It's a city of hills, lakes, and the Sound. Few sights are lovelier. We could hear our footsteps on the gravel. Sander sucked nervously on a tooth.

"I don't understand why I'm doing this," he said. "I hired on at the *Star* as a general-assignment dogface. Why am I doing this?"

"Probably boredom."

"Probably."

We stepped through a wet hedge and squatted at the corner of Anders's sloping lawn.

"How do you propose to tell the kitchen from the john with architecture like that?" he asked.

"I assume the toilet's in the john."

"Probably," he said again. "You're sure about your dope: nobody lives in there with him?"

"I'll have to take Powell's word for it. Let's get it over with."

We walked hunched over like two heavies in a bum movie. Sander started giggling.

"Shhhhh. Quiet for God's sake," I whispered.

"Shit, this is ridiculous."

I found a side door and took out my little box of lock picks. Sander looked impressed.

"You know how to use those things?" he whispered.

I nodded yes and went to work.

"Where?"

"Would you shut up? Sam taught me."

"Oh." He peered curiously over my shoulder.

One bar for tension. I inserted it and twisted. So far. The other to take the ridges one by one. The first depression. Stop. Okay. The second. Stop. Okay. The third. Stop. Still okay. Then a slide as the path trailed off.

"I think I've got it." I could feel sweat gathering on my forehead but I couldn't wipe it off. The thumb of my left hand began to ache from keeping the pressure on the pick. I felt an ominous trickle of sweat leave my eyebrow and knew in a minute it would be in my eye.

The lock wouldn't budge.

"What's the matter?" whispered Sander.

I withdrew the pick and shook the cramps from my fingers.

"I'll get her this time."

I tried. It wouldn't come. It was too much for me.

"It won't come."

"Why don't we just break a window?" Sander looked anxiously down the street. He was sweating as much as I was.

"Because he'll know we've been in here. The trick is to get what we need without him knowing it. Let's try another door."

"They'll all have the same kind of lock, won't they?"

He was right, but I didn't know what else to do. We eased around a corner to the back of the house. I tried another door; no use, it was the same lock.

"Why don't we just go through this window? It's not latched on the inside," said Sander. He grinned broadly.

He was right. It was unlatched and covered only by an aluminum screen held in place with flanges and wing nuts.

Sander removed the screen and in a minute we were inside a bedroom that was apparently never used. We were both trembling from nervous fatigue. We sat on the carpet listening to the sounds of the city far below. The rain had picked up again. We could hear it rustling the leaves.

"Christ, let's get on with it," Sander said after two minutes that seemed like two hours.

It was a gorgeous home; everything in it was in natural wood. There were lovely photographs of the Pacific Northwest on the walls. It looked like the set for a magazine layout, but I wouldn't want to live there. Our eyes had gotten used to the darkness outside. What was coming through the glass skylights enabled us to find our way around without using our flashlights. It didn't take long for us to find what we were looking for: Anders's study.

Its size was extraordinary for a study but there was no doubt that's what it was. The walls were lined with thousands of hardcover books.

"So this is where the review copies go." Sander shook his head.

I couldn't believe the number of books. It was awesome. "Do you suppose he ever reads any of these?" I asked.

"Hell no. I have it on good authority that he spends his time watching Godzilla movies on the tube. Watch this." Sander pulled a book at random from a shelf and opened it. "Never been cracked."

I tried one with the same result. "I believe you might be right."

Sander coughed once and muffled a second. "Look at this: the *Encyclopaedia Britannica* and the *Great Books* in genuine leather. I'll make book he doesn't know Machiavelli from Woody Herman. What he does, see, is leave the door casually ajar at parties so people on their way to take a leak will be encouraged to have a little peek and be impressed at the scholar-editor."

I opened my leather valise and removed a Polaroid camera with a flash attachment. "We're going through every drawer here in search of anything that has to do with stocks or securities of any kind. When you open a drawer, take a picture of the contents with this Polaroid. There is plenty more film in the valise. When you finish with a drawer, try to make it look the same as when you opened it. Just match the picture."

"Good sport," said Sander. He opened one drawer of Anders's teak desk. The camera flashed.

I opened a second and took my own picture.

We found letters from his daughters, letters from a sister in Richmond and a brother in San Diego, correspondence with newspaper editors with whom he had become personal friends, household bills, but nothing to do with investments, stocks, securities, or taxes. We did find a $3,500 estimate from a land-scape architect and a $14,000 estimate by an interior decorator, both recent. The decorator's reference to something "tastefully modern" draw a disgusted "shit!" from Sander.

"I want to go back," he said.

"What do you mean you want to go back? We've barely started."

"No, no, I mean back from this 'tastefully modern' crap. Maybe 1840 or 1923 or sometime. I don't know."

"I sometimes think the same thing myself. We wouldn't have liked it then either. In 1840 you'd have to be content with small talk on a porch with the girl's mother watching from a rocking chair. In 1923, you'd have to learn how to screw in a rumble seat."

"I don't think we're going to find anything in here."

"I don't either," I said.

We left the study to find Anders's bedroom, and on the way it occurred to me that Powell, a shrewd judge of character, had inflicted Sander on me to give me a dose of myself. I liked him, but I could see where he would wear on people after a while. He had worked so long with the bogus that he couldn't see anything else.

Anders's bedroom featured more natural wood interiors, teak furniture, and photographs on the walls. Even Sander admitted the photographs weren't bad.

"Let's check his dressers just to be sure," I said.

"More pictures?"

"Absolutely." I grabbed the Polaroid and opened the first drawer. Sweaters.

Sander took the second. "Shorts," he said. "Fruit of the Looms. He was never in the service."

"Briefs?"

I could see Sander nodding in the darkness. "Should wear boxers. I read in a magazine once where a man's testicles are the coolest part of his anatomy. Boxers let 'em dangle in the breeze."

There was another unused bedroom next to the one Anders slept in. On the other side of that was a darkroom. There was the ever present skylight over the entryway, which contained a dryer, so we still couldn't turn the lights on. The walls were covered with more photographs. We stepped through another door into a room equipped with sinks and a fluorescent timing clock on the wall. We were able to turn on the lights there and in yet a third room, which contained enlargers and equipment for processing prints. Anders had the best of everything in darkroom equipment. Black and white and color, so he could do it all.

Even Sander was slightly awed. "My God, would you look at this stuff."

"Cost a couple bucks. The clips said he's won prizes."

"Those must all be his pictures in the hall and in his bedroom." Sander peered closely at a color enlarger.

"He's good, no doubt of that."

"I've been in the newspaper business seventeen years and never learned how to shoot a picture. Would you just look at this stuff?"

We turned off the lights and retreated to the hall to consider our next move. We squatted on the carpet and listened to the rain beating on a glass skylight. I thought I heard a dull thump in the distance. A car door?

Sander heard it too. "What was that?" he whispered quickly.

"Shhh!" I put my finger to my lips.

Sander wasn't about to be quieted. "That was a car door. Who in the hell would be getting out of a car at this time of night?"

That sickening, clutching fear that had gripped us when we first entered the window had returned. I had a sinking, awful feeling in my stomach. My mouth was dry and the sweating returned. I knew Sander felt the same way. I could hear him breathing in the darkness.

"Maybe we should run for it," he whispered.

"If that's a cop out there, it's too late for that." We listened to the rain on the glass and waited. Five minutes passed, then ten. Nothing.

The pressure was getting to Sander's nerves. "Listen, maybe we should bag the whole business."

I ignored him. "Is that business true about Anders watching Godzilla movies?"

"It's true. He had a nephew from Richmond, Virginia, spend a summer here as an intern. The kid was full of stories about his uncle. He was only nineteen and we bought him off with six-packs."

"A guy makes money in stocks, he wants a place to relax so he can gloat over his profit. Anders spends his time shooting pictures and watching television. If we find his set, I'll bet we'll find what we're after."

"After you, Red Ryder."

I led the way down the hall. My shirt was wet with sweat and plastered to my back and stomach.

Sander was thinking about the same thing. "If a cop drives by, he'll smell us in here."

"Little sweat'll loosen your blackheads."

We eased our way through the kitchen, which featured a microwave oven, a Jenn-Air broiling unit, and a fireplace that could be rigged with a rotisserie. The living room also had a fireplace, more photographs on the walls, and elegant Scandinavian furniture in teak. We came at last to a room that featured an expensive slate pool table, shelves of books whose titles were chosen to suggest a man of civilized and catholic taste, a wet bar stocked with Johnnie Walker scotch, Wild Turkey bourbon, Beefeater's gin, and nearly everything else you could imagine. There were overstuffed easy chairs covered with soft leather. Overstuffed but fashionable.

But no television set.

"Where's the damned television?" Sander wanted to know.

"It's here but it doesn't fit his image as a man of letters. Try one of those panels."

Sander did.

There it was: a color Sony with remote control. I sat down in the easy chair directly in front of the set. This was the one chair in the room that was flanked on both sides by slender teak cabinets. The tops of the cabinets were inlaid with ceramic tiles intended to look like folk art. The cabinets served as coffee tables. There was a telephone on the left cabinet together with a machine that answered the phone and recorded messages in Anders's absence.

I punched the rewind button on the recorder and listened to Anders's messages. There were four calls. The first two were from golfing friends who didn't know Anders was out of town. The third was promising. The fourth was a dandy.

The one with promise was from someone named Andy: "This is Andy at Donalco, John. We have to make some decisions about Aberlon and Wysocki. Can you give me a call as soon as possible?"

The dandy was from Lennie Senn, the man who controlled pornographic movie houses, massage parlors, and "photography" studios in Seattle. "This is Leonard Senn, Mr. Anders. What you required is on its way. If you would like a visit from Carla again, please don't hesitate to call."

I looked at Sander. "What kind of business could John Anders possibly have with Lennie Senn?"

"Easy. Anders has been fighting Balkin and the board of directors for months over the issue of whether or not the *Seattle Star* should accept ads for porn theatres and sleaze joints. Anders says it's a matter of the First Amendment; if you're a newspaperman you have to stand by the First Amendment, he says. You have to take it all the way, accept the crap with the good stuff. Balkin and the board of directors don't object to the revenue from the ads but they're under pressure from clerics and chamber of commerce types not to present an image of Seattle as sleaze city—bad for families, bad for image."

"What happened?"

"Anders hired a professor at the University of Washington to do a little study. The question was which costs the paper more, canceled subscriptions by people who are offended by the ads or lost revenue if we refused to print them? If we're

91

looking strictly at economics, the professor said, we should carry the ads."

"And?"

"Balkin and the board gave it up as a bad cause. Charley Powell was on Anders's side. We all were in the city room."

"But it was Anders who led the noble free-speech campaign and hired the professor."

"Said he'd pay for the study out of his own pocket if the paper wouldn't spring for it."

"Whoa! Now Lennie Senn on the phone."

The cabinet drawers contained popular novels, a bottle of aspirin, a crossword puzzle dictionary, a paperback edition of the Guinness book of records, a copy of Nathanael West's *Miss Lonelyhearts,* and some cubes of blue cue chalk.

Sander was getting jumpy. "For God's sake, we know about Lennie Senn and the name of Anders's broker or whoever; let's get out of here."

I agreed. I thought we'd found what we were after.

It was approaching daylight when we climbed out of the window we had entered by and replaced the aluminum screen. It was still raining. We hurried across the wet grass, paused at the hedge, and trotted back to the Fiat. Actually we began trotting but were running at the end, we were so glad to be out of Anders's house. We had found what we were after. We were free.

I swore to myself I'd never do anything like that again.

Sander sprawled out in the front of the Fiat and took a deep breath.

"No more of that shit for me," he said. He stripped the rubber gloves from his hands and wiped his sweaty palms on his thighs.

"Looks like Arlo Daw is still having a good time."

"I don't think he ever stops."

"That's where the sound of the door came from," I said. I started the Fiat and we were on our way.

No more than three blocks later we passed a squad car from the Seattle police department. Adrenaline whipped through my body, twisting my insides. My hands began to shake.

The squad car pulled in behind us.

"Oh, God!" said Sander.

"For Christ's sake, don't look around."

"I told you we should have taken off. Those bastards were out there waiting for us to come out."

The squad car was right on our ass. "They're following us because it's five o'clock in the morning and we're tooling through a posh residential neighborhood. They're checking our plates against their hot sheet. When they find we're clean they'll leave us alone."

The blue light on top of the squad car began blinking.

Sander saw the reflection in the glass. He suddenly looked very middle-aged. I pulled over.

"I'll do the talking."

Sander said nothing.

One cop stayed in the squad car. The other came up beside the Fiat and motioned with his flashlight for me to roll the window down.

"May I see your driver's license. Take it out of your wallet, please."

I gave him my license.

"You were going thirty-five miles an hour in a twenty-five-mile zone back there, Mr. Denson. May I ask you what you and your friend are doing here at this hour of night?"

That was nonsense. I'd been extra careful not to break any traffic laws.

"My friend Bob Sander here and I are both reporters for the *Seattle Star*." I took a deep breath and cleared my throat nervously. "We were at a party given by Councilman Daw, who lives back there a way."

"You two have some press cards or something?"

We gave him our press cards. The cop looked at them with his flashlight.

"I recognize your by-line, Sander. You covered our negotiations with the city a while back."

"I do whatever the city desk says," Sander shrugged.

"Daw had himself a real wingding, eh?"

Sander gave the cop a suggestive grin.

The cop grinned back. "You two fellows take it easy now."
He went back to the squad car. He and his partner left us with
a whoosh and disappeared up the street.

Sander wiped the sweat off his forehead with the back of
his arm. "I hadn't known Daw and Anders were neighbors. You
know, the word is Lennie Senn supplies the girls for Daw's
parties."

11

I PICKED UP BOB SANDER on the way to work the next morning. I found out he slept on a Japanese mat on the floor of a studio apartment. He must have had a great love life. We had breakfast in a corner cafe and read the morning paper, Sander looking distracted.

When we got to the *Star*'s city room, Sander hunched over, weight on the balls of his feet, and looked squint-eyed around the room.

Shay looked disgusted. "I give up."

Sander grinned. "Cat burglars in Monaco. Heiresses' jewels and all that. Leaping from building to building. Moving like a shadow. Then it's back to the party, debonair, think Cary Grant and blondes with yum yums."

"What did you find?" asked Shay.

"Ahh, baubles and trinkets, pearls and diamonds," said Sander.

"We found a couple of recorded telephone calls that were interesting. One from his stockbroker or someone, the other from Lennie Senn."

"Lennie Senn?"

"Senn mentioned an Anders 'requirement,' whatever that is. He didn't say what. And he mentioned a woman named Carla. Do you know any women named Carla?"

"Not since I was in high school in Sacramento."

Charley Powell was suddenly at my side. He looked ghastly, pale; his hands trembled. He started to speak but nothing came. He looked at Shay, then at me, his lips parted slightly, then closed.

"What is it, Charley?" Shay put a slender hand on Powell's stooped shoulder and looked into the gray eyes with the black pouches.

"A call, there." He motioned to his desk, where a button on his telephone went blink, blink, blink. Someone was on hold.

Powell looked down at his slight paunch. "You know, Shay, I'm getting old. Maybe I should quit this business, raise a garden or something."

"Charley!" said Shay. Her voice rose slightly.

Powell looked at me and sighed. "There's a man there, on hold, says he's heard Wes Haggart was on the take before he was murdered. Wants to know if anybody here gives a damn."

"You tell him you'd be a few minutes?"

Powell nodded yes.

"Think he'll still be there?"

Powell nodded yes again. "He'll be there. People like that don't just go away."

"You were hoping Wes was onto Anders and I'd be able to pin Anders."

Powell shrugged. "I've always tried to do my damndest for my readers. But them? Anders and Balkin and the rest. All they do is count their goddamned nickels and demand that I account for every minute my reporters spend on a story. Yes, I wanted it to be Anders."

For Powell, going on the take was like throwing the world series. "Say it isn't so, Wes Haggart," I said.

"Sweet Jesus, yes, say it isn't so." If ever I had seen a man standing on the very edge, it was Charley Powell. He looked at me evenly. "I want you to be sure, Denson, absolutely sure. I don't want you to take this joker's word for anything; I don't

96

care who he is. I want to know exactly, and I mean exactly, what it was that Wes did or didn't do. We owe him that."

"I never take anybody's word in a situation like this," I said.

"He's a goddamn liar, Denson."

I shrugged. "Did he give you a name?"

"Willie."

"Just Willie?"

"That's all," Powell said absently. He looked at Shay, then at the technicians across the room.

I walked over to Charley's desk, where a yellow hold button blinked silently. On the other end was a man who could very well destroy the *Star*'s reputation. I picked up the receiver.

There was heavy breathing on the other end. Nothing more.

"Hello."

"To whom am I speaking, please?"

"John Denson."

There was a muffled, wheezing laughter. "Mr. Denson, the flaky private."

I give him an appropriately flaky laugh. "Fat Willie Fargo, the Sidney Greenstreet of Seattle snitches."

"The very same, Mr. Denson." More wheezing laughter.

Fat Willie was an infamous snitch. He sold information to everybody and anybody. The underworld knew he was a snitch but allowed him to survive. He had his uses. The cops knew he lied as often as not but supported him anyway. He had his uses. Fat Willie sold to the highest bidder.

"Charley Powell tells me you're a citizen calling with some helpful information, Mr. Fargo."

Fat Willie wheezed. "Tell me, Mr. Denson, are you still a private these days or are you a newspaper reporter? Your status is confusing."

"Is that your question, Willie, or someone else's?"

"Mine alone, Mr. Denson. I call the city editor of the *Seattle Star* with some information and I wind up with a man I know to be a private detective. It arouses my curiosity." No wheezing this time. Fat Willie was serious.

"I'm a reporter detailed to find out who murdered Wes Haggart and those two young women."

Fat Willie muffled a cough. "Well, I suppose it doesn't make

97

any difference. As you know, Mr. Denson, I circulate and listen. A tidbit here, a tidbit there, and I begin to wonder. During the last year or so I began hearing more and more about your wonderful Mr. Haggart. I finally put my tidbits together, and do you know what I found?"

"No, what's that?"

"That Wes Haggart was on the take, that's what I found."

I saw both Charley Powell and Shay watching me from Shay's desk. The technicians on the far side of the room had paused in their work and were relaxing with Styrofoam cups of coffee.

"Why are you calling us? Why don't you go to the police, Willie? They'd love to embarrass the *Star*."

Fat Willie really laughed this time. "The cops are nickel-and-dimers, Mr. Denson, you know that. They have to live by a budget. Your Mr. Balkin is a capitalist; he has real money."

"Let me guess: for a small sum, you'll be happy to leave your tidbits just as they are, tidbits."

"That's it, Mr. Denson, that's it. The sum is small really, just ten thousand dollars."

"Just what is it that Wes is supposed to have done, Willie?"

Fat Willie coughed again. "You're a corker, Mr. Denson, a real corker. That's what I have to sell. If I told you now, you'd start a cover."

"You understand the city desk doesn't have ten grand lying around in petty cash. I'll have to discuss this with John Anders and Harold Balkin."

"Bureaucrats are bureaucrats, Mr. Denson."

"I can't say how they'll react."

"When push comes to shove, Mr. Denson, they'll pay. Ten K is small to what it'll cost if I go to the cops."

What he said was true. Fat Willie held a pat hand.

"I'll need time, Willie," I said.

"One week, Mr. Denson, I'll get back."

"Just how strong is your dope, Willie?"

"Strong enough, Mr. Denson." Fat Willie wheezed and hung up.

I walked back to the desk where Shay and Charley Powell waited. I sat on the edge of the desk and watched the workmen unpack a VDT from a cardboard box. Like obstetricians, they were pulling the *Seattle Star* from the comforting womb of tradition.

"Well?" It was Shay. Powell said nothing.

"A man named Fat Willie Fargo," I said. "Always looked to me like Sidney Greenstreet."

"Who is Fat Willie Fargo?" asked Powell.

"A snitch, an informant. Fat Willie is the most famous in Seattle. The creeps in town know he's a snitch but they leave him alone because he's useful for an occasional red herring. Does that make sense?"

It did to Powell. Shay didn't seem so sure.

"Is it possible he could have the goods on Wes?"

"Entirely," I said.

"What does he have?"

"He won't say. Says it'll cost the *Star* ten grand to find out, otherwise it's the cops."

"How much time do we have?"

"One week."

Powell took a deep breath and closed his eyes. "Can we beat him to it?"

"That depends." I looked at Shay.

"On what?" she said.

"Keep in mind, I'm not asking that you take the first wave ashore at Omaha Beach. You'll survive, though maybe not as the same Shay you are now."

"Depends on what?"

Charley Powell picked up a pencil and began doodling on a piece of paper. "Tell her what you want, Denson."

I tried to avoid her eyes but I couldn't. "There is a banker somewhere in this town, he may be fat or skinny, married or single, charming or a jerk, I don't know, but there's one thing he has that we don't."

"What's that?" Shay took my blue eyes straight on.

"Access to Wes Haggart's savings account and checking account. If we can find out what's in there, we have a chance of beating Fat Willie."

"And if we don't?"

"Then maybe not."

Shay examined her manicured fingernails. "There's no other way?"

I shook my head. "Not that I know of."

"Done," she said.

Charley Powell squeezed her shoulder and returned to the city desk without saying a word.

"Hey listen, knucklehead, I know my men. All I'll have to do is lean a bit here, brush a thigh there, and act dumb."

"Jesus Christ, I hope so, Shay," I said. I realized that I might be asking her to do the same thing someone had asked of Samantha Becker. I hoped to God that Shay wouldn't get hurt.

It was time to find one of Lennie Senn's girls, the lady named Carla.

12

THE FIRST PLACE I TRIED was called "Mona's Photographer's Models" and was on the road to Sea-Tac Airport. Mona liked her name and had it painted huge and in hot pink. "Photographer's Models" was smaller and in Day-Glo chartreuse. Class all the way. Mona did without windows. Nobody was parked in the asphalt lot. A sign on the door said Mona accepted MasterCard, Visa, and American Express.

I stepped inside. A blonde looked up from watching "As the World Turns" on a small black-and-white television set that had a problem with snow.

"I can't marry Bob," said a girl on the tube.

"Just a second, I don't want to miss this," said the blonde.

The TV girl's male companion looked stunned. "You can't marry Bob?"

"No," said the girl. She was a looker. A tear formed on her cheek. The tear began to roll. So did the set. The blonde put it straight with a knob on the back.

"But why? Why?" said the man. He was a looker too. A stud.

"I can't tell you," said the girl.

"Goddamn," said the real-life blonde who was watching the set, transfixed. She adjusted the set again.

"You can't just skip out on the wedding without seeing Bob," said the stud on the screen.

"I can and I will. I don't have any choice," said the girl. She looked like she was on the very verge.

The young man looked understanding. "I'm your friend, Val, you can tell me." He looked tender.

"Is he going to play grab ass? Is that what's next?" I asked the for-real blonde who was caught up in all this.

The blonde glared at me.

"Are you my friend, Derek? Are you?" asked the girl on the set.

Derek took Val's hand. "I'm your friend, Val, and I'm Bob's. I'll do anything you ask. You know that. But you have to tell me why you aren't going through with the wedding."

Val looked stricken. The set began to roll.

"Fuck," said the real-life blonde. She adjusted the set once more.

"I found a letter from Bob to his parents open on his dresser. Derek, he hadn't told his parents or his sister about the wedding. He's, he's ashamed of me."

The camera moved in on Derek's face. He looked sincere and compassionate. There was suddenly an ad about floor wax. The blonde turned the sound down.

"No, he's not gonna play grab ass. We don't do that here either. We take all major credit cards and have cameras to rent. The girls are beautiful and professional."

Sure they were.

"I've got my own camera." I showed her my Nikon. "How many girls you got here this afternoon?"

The blonde was suddenly wary. "This is an on-the-level business. We provide professional models for serious art photographers."

"Look, I'm not a cop. I just like variety, that's all."

The blonde relaxed. The ad was off and a brunette and a woman with a perfect face were on the tube. The woman with a perfect face strode nervously back and forth with a letter in her hand.

"She's gone, Alice, gone. Bob is due here in a half an hour for his wedding and Val is gone."

"Just a minute," said my blonde hostess. She was satisfied I wasn't a cop.

"I don't understand. I just don't understand," said Alice. She looked concerned, but the viewer knew it was phony.

"Is Alice in love with Bob?" I asked the blonde.

"Shhh," the blonde silenced me with a finger to her lips.

"She didn't say why. She just said she was going and wouldn't be coming back. She said she wanted to get on with her life. Poor Val, my beautiful daughter," said the woman with the perfect face.

"That woman is Val's mother?" I couldn't believe it.

The blonde glared at me. "Would you shut up for Christ's sake?"

"Look, I just want to take some pictures."

"In a minute, in a minute."

The set began to roll. The blonde fiddled with the knob but it didn't work.

"Val has to live her own life, Andrea, you know that," said Alice. She put her arm around Andrea. Lesbians?

The blonde was content for the moment to watch a picture that went flip, flip, flip on the screen. Val, Bob, Derek, Alice, Andrea, they were all running together in my mind. The picture cured itself. There was a girl on the screen. It was maybe Val, maybe Alice, maybe Andrea. They were all gorgeous and all looked the same.

A rich, resonant male voice urged the viewers to turn in the next day for the next episode of "As the World Turns."

The blonde turned the set off.

"We've got a couple of brunettes back there. One thin, one with a pair, and then there's me. It'll cost you fifty bucks an hour. You name the pose, that's all you get. We don't sell extras. Half-hour minimum per girl."

"I'll start with the thin," I said.

She led me to a back room where there was a couch, a mat on the floor, and a blank wall.

"This ain't a set out of *Playboy,* but I'm sure you don't give

103

a damn. They've got nighties, transparent panties, and that sort of thing. If that's your taste. Helen!"

Helen appeared from behind a curtain wearing tight pants and a blouse with no bra. She looked like she'd been asleep.

"Got a customer," said the blonde. "How long'll you be?"

"I don't know. Not long. Then I'll be wanting the other."

"The one with the pair?"

"Her, sure."

"Watch the clock," said Helen, and the blonde disappeared into the waiting room. She turned on another soap opera.

"What's your pleasure?" said Helen. She stripped off her blouse and looked cold. She had goose bumps on her breasts.

"Is Helen your real name?"

"Honey, I've had a lot of names. Want me to take my pants off?"

"You're fine. Have you ever called yourself Carla?"

"I've had a bunch but never Carla." She grinned. "You have a thing on women named Carla?"

I shrugged. "Some like ropes, some like showers. I like Carlas."

"Oh boy!" Helen shook her head.

"Listen, that's okay. Can you send in the other girl?"

Helen looked alarmed. "Did Rose tell you it's a half-hour minimum?"

I nodded. "This is extra." I gave her twenty bucks of the *Star*'s money. "You know any Carlas in this business?"

"Knew one in Houston a couple years ago." Helen put her blouse back on and disappeared without a word. The girl with a pair replaced her with extra enthusiasm. She had heard about the twenty and immediately began peeling clothes. Before I could stop her she had stripped completely and was looking coyly at me over her shoulder, her rear end jutting out in what can charitably be described as a provocative manner. It was awful.

"How's this?" she asked.

"Just hold it." I fiddled with my camera for a second. "Say, what's your name?"

"Carla!" she said eagerly.

"Helen tell you to say that?"

104

"Oh no!" She was lying. She had also assumed a pose that was awkward to hold. The effort was getting to her but she knew about Helen's twenty and was not about to break. She was like a Marine recruit standing at attention. She began to sway visibly.

"Do you know of any Carlas in this business besides you? Here in Seattle, I mean."

"I don't know any Carlas," she said. She spread her thighs slightly in an effort to give me some pink.

I snapped a shot to give her a break. "That's okay," I said.

She came out of it cheerfully but I knew her thighs and back were aching. I think she was having second thoughts about all this being worth it. What if I didn't tip her as I had Helen?

"Do you want another one like that?"

"That's okay," I said. I gave her a twenty also.

The word was out, and when the blonde came she was determined to outdo the others. She discarded her clothes with abandon and sprawled suggestively on the couch.

"Don't know any Carlas but how's this?"

I looked disappointed. "I gotta have a Carla." I gave her a twenty. She went for it like a largemouth bass, totaled my time, and billed me.

"You didn't do too much in the way of shooting pictures, troop, but good luck anyway." She was thinking I was a grand rip.

The afternoon rush hour was beginning when I started back into town. It took me a while to get to the second "art studio." This one was Monique's; the sign again was enormous and in hot pink. "Photographer's Models" was smaller and in chartreuse, just like before. I was dealing with the McDonald's of Seattle porn. While people weren't beating in the doors to get in, the labor was cheap and overhead low. There was no maintenance to speak of.

Apparently all you need to go into business is a couple of girls and a black-and-white television set. The receptionist at Monique's was watching the tube also. She was watching a game show and looked up at me with tired, experienced eyes.

The master of ceremonies on the set was charming, flirtatious, had a rich voice, perfect teeth, and never stopped smiling. A woman contestant, a housewife from Philadelphia, giggled like she was freaked on hallucinogens.

The girl with the tired eyes turned the set off with disgust. "Christ, what bullshit!" she said. "What do you need?"

I didn't want to have to go through the same depressing routine as at Mona's, so I tried a new line. I pulled five crisp twenties from my wallet.

"I'm looking for a girl named Carla. I think she might work in one of these places or maybe a massage parlor here in town. I'm not a cop. No one's in trouble."

The tired eyes glazed over. There was genuine fear there. "And mum's the word," I added.

She looked at the hundred, then at me. "Who are you?"

I shrugged my shoulders. "What does it matter?" I pulled another five of the *Star*'s twenty-dollar bills from my wallet.

"It matters a whole lot, chum."

"I'm a private. I'm working for a client in Portland. His daughter ran away last fall. She has a boyfriend in a motorcycle gang that roams around the Northwest. She worked in a massage parlor in Portland for a while. He wants me to check out Seattle for him."

She shrugged. "It doesn't matter. I don't know of any Carlas anyway." She looked at me. "Even if I did, I wouldn't tell you; it could get me hurt."

"You should try waitressing."

She clearly thought I was a little slow. "Waitressing's degrading and doesn't pay anything. I've got one hell of a body. Figured it was just sitting around, why not use it? I don't see what the big deal is. It's flattering to have somebody pay fifty bucks an hour to take pictures of me. What's it hurt?"

"It doesn't, I guess."

"I don't fuck 'em, bub, if that's what you're thinking."

"I didn't say that."

"And if you don't think I have a great-looking body, part with fifty out of Fort Knox there and I'll show you what I mean."

Everybody has to take pride in his work, I thought. I almost took her up on it. "You don't know any Carlas?"

106

"Not a one, honey."

"Thanks a lot then. Maybe I'll come back to shoot pictures someday."

She grinned. I took my money and left.

The third place I tried was "Marianne's." It looked like the franchise was limited by the number of women's names that began with an *M*. When I opened the door there was a girl sitting there looking frozen. The television set was not running.

Something was wrong. Very wrong.

I slammed the door and took off like a wide receiver on a fly pattern.

A man (was it men?) shouted at me. I leaped into the Fiat and all 1,300 of those marvelous cc's came to life the first try. There was a tremendous explosion. Glass all over the place. I couldn't think. I looked at the hair on the back of my wrist. The back of my neck began to sting like hell.

I put it in reverse and tromped on it. The Fiat shot backward.

There was a sickening crunch and a man went sprawling into the street. An automatic pistol slid across the asphalt like a wayward hockey puck. I turned to the right.

The muzzle of a pistol.

Behind that, a man.

I dove for the seat.

Another explosion. The passenger's window shattered. My foot slipped off the accelerator. I couldn't find it.

Sweet Jesus!

The front windshield came apart under yet a third round of pistol fire.

I opened the door on the street side so I could see without raising my head. Felt like a movie redskin keeping his pony between himself and the cavalry Winchesters. I found the accelerator with my hand and redlined the tac in reverse. The 1,300 cc's screamed in pain. The Fiat fishtailed crazily. Man and machine went sideways around the corner.

I stomped on the brake with my knee and scrambled back up on the seat.

The heavy appeared around the corner.

I almost lost my transmission forcing it into low gear.

The heavy was jamming a new clip into the butt of his pistol.

I wondered what I would tell my insurance agent. I aimed right at the heavy and popped the clutch. His eyes got wide. He dove for cover. The right rear of my Fiat bounced off the corner of the brick building.

I missed the heavy but kept going.

Blue smoke rolled from the Pirelli radials on the front.

I redlined it in low gear, then forced it into second. Then third. I made it. I was alive.

13

NOT MORE THAN THREE BLOCKS later I heard the siren. My rearview mirror contained two pencil-shaped shards of glass but I saw it anyway: a squad car bearing down on me through the traffic.

I pulled over.

While I sat there waiting, the sweat began to come. My hands started trembling.

"Get out of the car please," a voice said.

"What?" I turned. It was a cop. I'd forgotten about the police.

"Would you get out of the car please," the cop said.

I watched his mouth move. It was hard to connect the words with the lips.

"Oh," I said. I fumbled with the door but it was too much. My hands were spastic. I felt a warm trickle on the back of my neck. "Blood," I said stupidly.

"I see that," said the cop. He opened the door. "Wait right there, don't move."

He was gone.

I could hear voices. Numbers. A man's voice. A woman.

She had a nice voice. The man's again. The woman. More numbers. I wanted to stop shaking but I couldn't.

"We'll have an ambulance in a few minutes." It was the cop again. He had a blanket in his hand and a pillow.

"Where did you get the blanket?" It seemed important to know where he got the blanket. I didn't hear what he said because I started vomiting. I lurched out onto the street and fell down. I couldn't stop vomiting.

Somebody grabbed me by the shoulder. I kept vomiting until my throat burned and I got cramps in my ribs. There wasn't anything down there but still I vomited.

"What happened?" a voice said.

"Stand back."

"What happened to him?" the voice persisted.

"I said stand back! Everybody stand back, he'll be okay."

Hands were wrapping the blanket around my shoulders as I hunkered in the street on all fours, caught in desperate spasms of dry vomiting. I pushed the hands away. I didn't want to get blood on the blanket.

It was a cop. A cop had the blanket. I wanted to tell him I didn't want to screw up his blanket. It belonged to the taxpayers. I wanted to tell him nothing like this ever happened to Philip Marlowe. But I couldn't tell him. I just heaved.

Then the heaving stopped, suddenly, mercifully.

Then I couldn't breathe. My mouth was dry, and I couldn't get enough air. Hands were on my arms pulling me to the side of the street.

"Lay down here," said the cop.

It should be lie down, I wanted to tell him. There were people watching. Faces.

"I'll get blood on your blanket," I said at last. It felt good to say it.

I was on my back, on damp grass. The cop put the pillow under my feet and wrapped me up in the blanket. There was blue sky up there. No clouds.

"What happened?" a voice said.

"Will he be all right?"

All those questions and there I was ruining a wool blanket that belonged to the city of Seattle. Why didn't they ask about the blanket? They had paid for it. Officer, does he have to bleed on our blanket? A handkerchief wiped my forehead, which was wet with sweat.

Suddenly there was a young man in a white outfit bending over me. He put the palm of his hand on my forehead and took my wrist with his thumb and forefinger.

"Okay, pal, it's gonna be okay now."

I wanted to thank him for being in such a humane profession but nothing came. My brain wanted to thank him but my mouth couldn't turn the trick.

Suddenly my mouth worked. "Tell the cop guys were shooting at me."

"We know." It was the cop. He was standing right behind the young man in white.

"I was just trying to get away. I think I backed over one of them."

"That'll all wait. You take it easy now," said the cop.

The man in white pulled back the sleeve of my shirt and slid a hypodermic needle into my arm. "This is good stuff, man, you'll like it a lot," he said.

He had a point. It stopped the shakes. A warm glow spread over my face. It was nice.

"Thanks," I said.

I felt them lift me up. I closed my eyes and surrendered to the drug.

The first thing I saw when I woke up was a man in his mid thirties dressed in a pinstriped three-piece suit. He was absolutely immaculate, everything about him. The white shirt was perfect. The knot in his tie just right. The straight blond hair was fashionably cut over his ears. He was talking to a medical doctor, an older man, who deferred to him.

The man in the three-piece suit was Roy Hofstadter, county prosecutor.

A nurse, whom I hadn't seen, apparently noticed I was awake and cleared her throat.

The medical doctor looked my way, looked back at Hofstadter for a cue, and Hofstadter motioned for him to check me out.

The doctor had ears that stuck out and a small nose that

turned up. I could see inside his nostrils. "My name is Dr. Maurice Fitzpatrick. You've sustained minor skin lacerations on the back of your . . ."

"You mean I was cut by flying glass," I interrupted.

"Yes, and you went into shock. But you'll be fine now. Mr. Hofstadter would like to ask you some questions."

"Who's Mr. Hofstadter?" I asked, and watched the county prosecutor.

That was a vicious question for a man of Hofstadter's ambition. He colored visibly.

Dr. Fitzpatrick looked momentarily confused. "Mr. Hofstadter is the county prosecutor."

"He knows who I am," said Hofstadter.

"Does he have to talk to me now?" I asked, ignoring Hofstadter's remark.

The good doctor wished he was out of the combat zone. "I won't see any reason why not."

Hofstadter dismissed the doctor and the nurse with a barely perceptible motion of his head. "Would you send my stenographer in, please."

He would have preferred to work alone but he needed a witness. A redhead entered the room with a tape recorder.

"I want it taped and I want you to take notes as well."

The redhead, a nicely rounded woman in her early thirties, nodded yes.

Hofstadter regarded me carefully. He thought he was better than other people. He knew what was best for them. He was smarter. He was better looking. He was successful. He wanted more success. He had had his way in the past. He wanted to have it in the future. He was looking at John Denson, a small person as people go. Hofstadter knew, from an instinct that had served him well, that this John Denson was very likely the key to his becoming governor or United States senator. He wanted that more than anything else in the world. And if he were elected senator, why who knows what might happen then? A bright, good-looking young man from the West. He did very well on television. Women trusted him. Men thought he was tough and smart.

Since Hofstadter was smart, he had gotten the book on this

John Denson from Denson's friends at the police station. The cops had told him Denson was a randy flake, honest, intelligent, an eater of raw cauliflower, a drinker of cheap red wine, a bit of a cynic, a romantic. The cops told Hofstadter to be careful.

Hofstadter had too much to lose not to be careful.

I eyed the redhead; five to one she wanted me to take him down a notch. She was a good one though, kept it to herself.

Hofstadter looked at the back of his hand. The fingernails were just right. "Mr. Denson, are you a private detective or an employee of the *Seattle Star?*"

"Both."

"Both?" He raised his eyebrows. "Would you explain that, please?"

"I went back to the newspaper business this week but I still want to do some detective work. Good moonlight. Newspaper publishers are stingy."

It was clear he didn't believe that one. "Are you on a case right now?"

"Yes."

"Who is your client?"

I looked him straight in the eye. "As you know, I'm not required to tell you that."

"What newspaper story are you working on?"

"I'm working on two. I'm trying to find out if a wholesale food outfit burned its own warehouse. And I'm trying to find out if a Japanese multinational corporation named Matsumura Industries is the angel of the Slackwaters in that salmon-fishing mess."

Hofstadter looked irked. That's what Charley Powell had told him.

"I'm also trying to beat you guys to Wes Haggart's murderer."

He looked even more irked.

"But I suppose Charley Powell told you that."

Hofstadter looked sullen.

The redhead looked his way without moving her head. She was loving every minute of it.

"What were you and Bob Sander doing in the Queen Anne Heights area at five A.M. this morning?" Hofstadter ran his tongue over his teeth. He had played an ace.

113

"We weren't at Councilman Daw's party, as you know. We were returning from a rendezvous with a very married lady and her equally married girlfriend."

He was good at concealing his disappointment. "Who were they?"

"It's a small town, Mr. Hofstadter. The ladies value their privacy."

"Would you prefer to answer the question before a grand jury?"

He wasn't as good as he thought he was. "Before a grand jury, yes. For you, no."

"When were you assigned to investigate the Wes Haggart matter?"

"The Wes Haggart murder? The morning after he was killed."

Hofstadter smiled. He didn't see anything funny but he smiled. If a shark could smile that's what it would look like.

"I want you to tell me what happened to you this afternoon."

The stenographer swallowed. She knew the background of the shoot-out.

"Some guys chased me and started shooting at me with pistols. I jumped into my Fiat, backed over one of them, backed around a corner, tried to run over a second but missed, and beat hell out of the speed limit trying to get out of there. Your cop stopped me and I started puking and shaking."

The redhead looked at the floor.

Hofstadter moved slightly closer to the bed. "Why did they choose you to shoot at?"

"Because I was trying to trace a woman who might work in a sleaze joint. I had asked questions at two places earlier, one by Sea-Tac Airport and another called Monique's. This was my third try. Dumb. Those guys were gangsters. They wanted to know why."

"So do I."

"So do you what?"

"Want to know why."

"Sometimes Charley assigns me stories. Sometimes I scrounge. If you really have to know, I was scrounging at five A.M. this morning and again this afternoon."

114

The redhead looked interested. Hofstadter thought he was close to a kill.

"Scrounging for what?"

"I was trying to find out if the people who run those joints supply girls for Councilman Arlo Daw's parties. I've heard Daw and Lennie Senn are pals."

I'm not sure, but I thought Roy Hofstadter stopped breathing for just a second. He looked at the redhead. She waited with her pen. Her face was a perfect mask.

"I think that will be all this afternoon." Hofstadter turned and without another word left the room.

I winked at the redhead. "Buy you a drink sometime."

"Sure," she said.

"What happened to the guy I ran over?"

"His friend picked him up and threw him into a Chrysler. They disappeared."

"That was a neat trick. Must have been cops all over the place."

The redhead picked up her tape recorder and left.

A nurse came in a few minutes later to check the dressing on the back of my neck. She was a capable-appearing person in her fifties.

I sat up to help her out and my neck hurt.

"I heard you were the person involved in the shoot-out this afternoon."

"You heard?"

"On the radio. Witnesses said you backed over one of them in your little car and you tried to run over the other but ran into a building instead."

"Did the radio say what happened to the blanket?"

The nurse looked puzzled.

"The blanket the cop wrapped me up in. For some screwy reason I kept worrying that I'd ruin it with my blood. I wonder what happened to it."

"Your neck's okay. They'll probably let you out of here in a couple of hours. That blanket bit was the crazies. You were in shock."

"I'd still like to know about the blanket."

The nurse ignored me. She went about her business.

115

Charley Powell and Shay stopped by a little while later. Powell looked embarrassed. Shay looked, well, what can I say? There are a few times in a man's life when he really needs a Shay. For me this was one of them. She knew that. She also knew I'd never admit it.

"I tried to smuggle you a pint but they said no," said Powell. "Are you okay?"

I nodded yes. "My neck's fine. The bad part was just after I escaped those guys; I freaked out. Never had anything like that happen before."

Shay was smiling but getting a little emotional too. That was nice.

"I've been thinking about beating you at pool," I said. "I think my problem is concentration. I have to learn to concentrate."

Shay squeezed my hand but didn't say anything. That made Powell even more embarrassed. How can a guy be a tough city editor when he gets sentimental over a little affection?

"Listen, why don't you two get a doctor and my pants. Let's the three of us get out of here and take a walk in the rain or something."

They got my pants and we went for our walk. It was drizzling slightly, more like a wet mist than a rain. I was alive and felt marvelous. Shay and Charley Powell were strangely silent for having sprung a man who escaped an ambush alive and was now striding grandly through the drizzle. Something was wrong.

"Ah yes, this rain feels good. You found your way to the banker's heart, didn't you, Shay?"

She tightened her grip on my arm. "I didn't have to swap my rear, either."

"Well, hell then, why the gloom?" I knew the reason for the gloom. We faced our moment of truth striding briskly, three abreast, a middle-aged city editor, a lovely young woman, and a flake named Denson. We kept moving.

It was Powell who spoke next: "The gloom, Denson, is Wes Haggart's checking account."

I suspected as much. "Oh boy, what is it?"

Shay leaned her head on my shoulder. "Wes Haggart has

116

been living on credit for five or six years now; he didn't have ten cents in savings. All of a sudden, six months ago, he began depositing five thousand dollars a month in his checking account. At the beginning of the next month he started transferring the five thousand to a savings account separate from his usual savings account, which remained empty as usual. He went through that routine six times before he was murdered."

"Wes Haggart was a Harry," Charley Powell said. He had given up.

"Not necessarily," I said.

"That locks it up, doesn't it?"

"No," I said. No sense telling Charley so, but it sure as hell looked that way.

"Anything else?" Shay asked.

"Did he ever draw on his separate savings account?"

"No," she said. "Why do you ask?"

"Just wondered," I said.

15

MY NECK WAS SORE but it was okay. I got a haircut to move my hairline up a tad where the hospital had shaved my neck to remove some glass. Then I rented a Ford Fiesta. I spent two hours on the streets of Seattle making sure I wasn't being followed, then I found a hotel for Shay and myself. We drank a six-pack of beer and watched Johnny Carson's monologue, after which we slipped into one another's arms. It had been a long week and a hard day but Shay was something special.

I made a stiff-necked appearance in the city room the next day. There was a letter in my notebox. It had been hand-delivered, not mailed. I broke the seal and read it:

Dear Mr. Denson:

We apologize for your unfortunate experience yesterday. We don't fear the police. The police are toothless and we beat them in the courts. But we don't like publicity; it encourages the righteous. Our people just wanted to find out what you were up to. When you

ran like that—why they're young and eager to show
their skills. You understand. However, if you have in
mind any sort of exposé, they'll be back. Your mistake
was in thinking you could buy Frieda off. You should
have taken her picture. You offended her. The man you
ran over has a fractured pelvis. Serves him right.

I hardly expected a signature. There wasn't one. I pocketed
the note and sat down to write a story, in the first person, in
which I tried to convince my readers that I had been assaulted
in broad daylight, for no apparent reason, by two mobsters
with pistols blazing.

Sander read it standing over my shoulder going hee, hee,
hee.

Shay asked him what was the matter.

"You really expect the reader to believe that crap?" he
asked me.

"Powell says we gotta have something. My name was all
over the radio yesterday. The readers will expect something."

Sander grinned one of his odd grins. "The people on the
tube didn't make it there in time for all the puking and good
stuff. Had to settle for close-ups of glass on the street and a
bloody blanket. Must have really pissed 'em."

So that's what happened to the blanket. The taxpayers got
a ride out of their blanket after all. Money well spent.

"Was it nice and wet still or had it started to crust over?"
I asked.

"Naw, a pretty boy reporter held it in his hand and it
drooped pretty convincingly. He probably peed on it before
they shot the film. He said the streets of urban America can
sometimes be a violent place." Sander looked very serious. "He
said, 'We've seen that here, today, in our town.' "

"Wow, heavy stuff," Shay said, and looked as wide-eyed as
she could.

"I thought we might hear the theme from *The Godfather* but
we didn't, we got an ad for a 'women's sanitary' product. A
young girl wanted to play tennis with a handsome young stud
but she couldn't. She switched brands and the next thing we

see she's making out with the guy in the front seat of a Corvette. She's pooped from having played tennis all day but she's happy."

"Oh, shut up Sander," said Shay.

Sander went hee, hee, hee again and drifted back to his desk.

I filled out an expense account form:

"One each Fiat, Model 128, four-door, with Pirelli radials, AM-FM radio, tachometer."

I gave it to Powell. He looked at me in disbelief.

"Make sure it gets to Harold Balkin; he'll pay," I said.

"What do you do now?" He didn't blink at the reference to Balkin.

"I find out whether or not Wes Haggart was a Harry. I find out what he was up to. I find out who killed him. I find out if John Anders is a Harry. I find out if those mobsters have anything to do with him. I might even add Roy Hofstadter to the list. What does he have to do with the mobsters?"

Powell shook his head.

"That shouldn't be too hard," I said. "Look what we have to work with. A flaky detective, a hundred-and-five-pound blonde, and a cynic who's losing the hair on the front of his head."

"That isn't all Sander's lost," Powell said.

"He can feel still, beneath that."

Powell looked across the city room where Sander was staring into space and writing a story without looking at his typewriter. Sander paused, looked at his notebook, thought a moment, and continued writing. "He was married fifteen years; can you imagine living with that?"

"Not my style," I said.

"What do you do next?"

"Check out all the possibilities and hope those heavies think they frightened me off the scent."

Powell sighed. "Do me a favor and don't get Shay mixed up with those guys. You do that and I'll break your damned neck."

"I won't," I said. I had no intention of getting Shay mixed up in something she couldn't handle. "You keep her busy on

120

newspaper work this afternoon. I've got some legwork to do."

Powell nodded. "Shay!" he shouted.

I didn't wait to hear her argue that she should come with me. I headed for police headquarters.

I went to Captain James Gilberto, head of internal security. Gilberto owed me a favor. I had tracked down his runaway sixteen-year-old daughter who was whacked out on dope and screwing both genders because that was fashionable. His own cops hadn't been able to find her.

Gilberto knew something was up when I stepped into his office.

He looked at me suspiciously. "Denson. I see by the five-thirty news where they scared the pee out of you. Made a good yarn for those two cops. Halstead, I think one's name was."

Hell of a story for popcorn and draft beer. "Dandy for you sadists."

"Looks like you've survived to me."

"Payoff time, Jim."

Gilberto turned up the palms of his hands. "I don't know anything."

"You know how Fielding Enterprises plugged the news of its arson stunt a few months back."

Gilberto looked surprised. "That doesn't have anything to do with those jerks who tried to plug you."

"Didn't say it did."

Gilberto thought it over. "This stays here?"

"Certainly."

"It was a cop, but I don't want to give you his name. A decent guy up to his ass in debt so he took some on the side."

"I don't need his name," I said.

"Oh!" Gilberto looked surprised.

I looked blank. "And please tell your friend that being ambushed by two morons with pistols isn't like Steve McQueen in the movies."

"I'll do that." Gilberto grinned.

"Incidentally, who's in charge of vice these days?"

Gilberto was an honest man. He was loyal to his wife and did the best he could to raise good kids. It wasn't his fault his daughter went screwy; she was no different than a lot of others her age, caught by the rhetoric that drew them onto the rocks. Poor Gilberto. "Vice is Baird these days. Captain Louis Baird."

"Louis Baird?"

"You go far these days if you're the brother-in-law of the county prosecutor." Gilberto said it as a matter of fact. He seemed neither envious, alarmed, nor surprised.

"*Captain* Baird?" I didn't think Baird shaved yet.

"That's it."

I tried not to look drifty, but Gilberto wasn't dumb.

"We all know you and Sander were poking around Councilman Daw's latest wingding. Of course Roy Hofstadter knows about it. We all do. Daw sees to it we get what we ask for. We gotta eat, Denson; we can't all be romantics like you."

"Where would I go to find a girl named Carla, a girl Lennie Senn may have used to sweeten the pot in a business deal?"

"You're thinking of one of Arlo Daw's parties."

"It occurred to me."

Gilberto had recently gotten a nice pay raise. All Seattle cops had gotten them, due in large part to the clout of Arlo Daw. "Why pick on Arlo? He's just a guy who likes to have a good time. He's got the bucks. Why shouldn't he?"

"Would you believe me if I told you I don't give a damn about Arlo Daw?"

Gilberto's eyebrows raised slightly. "Scout's honor?"

"Scout's honor."

"Who gets hurt?"

I shrugged. "I don't know. Maybe Roy Hofstadter."

The cops didn't like Roy Hofstadter. Cops want crooks in jail. Hofstadter was interested in votes.

"Hmmmm," said Gilberto.

"I want to talk to Carla, that's all. On another matter."

"How do you propose to do that?"

"I want an invite to Arlo Daw's next party. Tell him I'm a randy bachelor who kept a police brutality case out of the *Star*. You're grateful."

Gilberto thought about it. "I'll think about it," he said.

"Call you back?"

"Call me back."

I started to leave, then stopped. "You might include Bob Sander too. Tell them he helped in the squash. Tell them it's a good idea to have someone on the *Star* who's, what's the word? Compromised."

"Bought off," said Gilberto.

"Right. There's plenty to go around at those parties from what I've been told."

Gilberto grinned. "We're not really on the take, you know. Makes Daw feel young. What's it hurt?"

"Doesn't, I guess."

"He scratches ours; we scratch his."

"Two of us, Sander and me," I said, and left.

The clouds had miraculously disappeared. The sun was out. The sky was blue. Mount Rainier was there, crisp and sparkling white against the blue. On a day like that there is no city more beautiful than Seattle. I took a little hike. I believed Gilberto about the Fielding Enterprises buy-off. The question now was whether it was a red herring. If it was, whose was it? Who was supposed to be diverted? I wandered through Pike's Market to look at the piles of salmon and stacks of fresh vegetables. The price of vegetables was way down. They had those plump little carrots, sweet jobs, not a hint of bitterness. The bell peppers were a rich green, crisp, sweet, and cheap to boot. Got myself some carrots, peppers, a small head of cauliflower, and headed back to the office.

I quartered and seeded the peppers with my pocketknife. Shay was out and I missed her. Anders passed by and paused to watch me eating green pepper.

"What are you doing?"

"Eating green pepper."

"I can see that, but why?"

I looked concerned. "Is there a management rule against it?"

"It isn't that," said Anders. "Four Roses I can understand. Green peppers are something else. Are you making any progress?"

"After I finish this pepper I'm going to call a cop who's going to invite me to one of Arlo Daw's parties."

123

Anders looked surprised. "Was Wes Haggart mixed up with that gang?"

"I don't know," I said.

Anders shook his head and disappeared into his office. I called Captain Gilberto. "Councilman Daw isn't sure," he said.

"About what?"

"He said people go there to, uh, do something a bit different. They got a right to privacy, he said."

"What kind of assurance does he need?"

Gilberto cleared his throat. "Mine. If anything gets in the paper, my career comes to a bloody, screeching halt."

"You've got my word."

"I should have my head examined, but okay. Daw's libido is apparently working overtime. He said you and Sander should show up around ten o'clock tomorrow."

"Thanks, Jim."

"Denson?"

"Yes."

"Eat your oysters."

The next day would be my sixth day at the *Seattle Star,* a good day to get some sleep and think things over.

14

ARLO DAW LIVED IN a two-story home of a modified
colonial architecture that is common on the East Coast but
rarely seen in the West. It was painted white and had green
shutters and a handsome portico with four grand columns.
Sander and I showed up fashionably late at 11 P.M. There was
apparently activity both upstairs and down. We listened for a
couple of minutes to some nice swing music on Daw's expensive stereo setup before I rapped the brass knocker on the
enormous doors of his home.

I swayed to the music. "It brings back memories, doesn't it?
You always want to go back to the music of your generation."

Sander understood. "What's that, Benny Goodman?"

"I don't know. You get to hold a girl, though. I never could
get used to dancing by myself."

"Nuzzling her neck's civilized foreplay," Sander said. "Kids
now think they're Africans or something."

A redhead opened the door. "Yes?"

"John Denson and Bob Sander," I said.

"Just a minute, please." She closed the door.

Sander rolled his eyes. "Jesus Christ!"

The door opened. Councilman Arlo Daw welcomed his guests. "Ah, Mr. Denson." He hesitated. He didn't know who was who.

I held out my hand.

"And you must be Bob Sander. I've seen your by-line many times. You do good work."

Arlo Daw was in his early fifties, a small man, not over five foot three and 120 pounds. He had white hair, a nose that was too big for his face, and wore a David Niven mustache. He was well known to anybody who had spent any time in Seattle. He knew power and liked it.

Daw took me by the elbow and guided me into the room. There was activity upstairs but Daw pointedly ignored that. He let us know, without being obvious, that we were part of the downstairs crowd. "Captain Gilberto tells me you saved the arse of some of our cops who got a little fancy."

"Did a number on some intoxicated Indians down by Pike," I said.

"Drunk Indians, you mean."

"That's what I mean."

"Gilberto tell you my rules?"

I nodded.

"I wouldn't buy Gilberto's song and dance from a snake-oil salesman. But he gave me an idea. The rules stand. I have my own reason for wanting you two here."

I grinned. "I thought as much."

Daw waved his arm generously. "You're welcome to anything you see. And I do mean anything." He winked. He grabbed a passing brunette by the elbow. Doe-eyed, I guess describes her. Like Shay's, the top button of her blouse was fashionably undone. "This is Helena. John Denson. Bob Sander."

Sander made his usual move to his left, trying to catch a nipple. Daw was onto him. "Helena, perhaps you would like to chat with Mr. Sander." He grinned and left to mingle with a crowd of fifteen to twenty people helping themselves to his booze, chatting in groups of two and three, and dancing to his extraordinary sound system.

Sander leaned my way: "Can you imagine that little bastard

on one of these broads, like a flea trying to fuck an elephant."

Helena overheard. She clucked her tongue disapprovingly but grinned the whole while. "You better not let the councilman hear you say that."

I left Sander with Helena clinging to his elbow. He clearly had never had a girl that lovely pay attention to him in his entire life. He knew she was salaried but he was flattered nevertheless, and a little embarrassed. He liked it. He had had his ups and downs; Helena was good for him. I wondered if Daw had sensed that; if he had, he wasn't all bad.

I helped myself to three fingers of Johnnie Walker scotch tempered only slightly by water. It was a mistake. I was a beer and wine man. Scotch would be onto me before I knew what happened. I should have known that. I had another. Sander was dancing close with Helena. Daw was telling dirty jokes to a small group that laughed at everything he said.

I admired the watercolors on Daw's walls. They were better than Anders's photographs. Watercolors captured truth and little more. A photograph told all, yet nothing.

A few minutes later I found her. Or rather she found me. She was in her early twenties, had rich auburn hair and a soft, sensuous figure that would ripen and perhaps hip out at age thirty-five.

"Hello, Carla's my name," she said. Carla. Just like that.

"John Denson. Are you a regular here, Carla?"

She smiled. "Mr. Daw seems to like me."

Carla was a sad, doomed sexual object, a casualty of our times. She should love and be loved. It wasn't right that anything could have gone so terribly wrong for such a lovely creature. I bit my lip and began to get emotional. Maybe it was the scotch, I don't know.

"Are you all right, Mr. Denson?"

I took a deep breath. "I'm okay, just thinking. John's my name."

"John, then." She drew near me. I could smell her perfume. I wanted to shake her and ask why, why, why?

But I didn't. I leaned against her, took her hand, and squeezed it. Her hand was soft and she responded. I thought of Shay. With Shay, it was right.

127

Yet there was a sharing. Her eyes told me she understood.

"I have an idea you're a nice person, Carla."

"I would like to be someday," she said. She squeezed my hand. She wasn't Shay but she too needed love.

What did it hurt?

"Shall we dance?" I asked.

We danced. We were the only ones who were dancing, but it didn't make any difference. She burrowed her face into my shoulder. I watched Arlo Daw over her shoulder.

"How do I get in touch with you in the future?" I asked her.

She spoke without unburrowing her face: "You'd best off do what you have in mind tonight, Mr. Denson."

"Oh?"

"I'm for hire."

"I know that."

"I'm very expensive. It's on the house tonight, so to speak." She said it as a matter of fact.

"I'm sorry this happened to you."

"You're not going to take me to bed, are you?"

"I don't think so."

"You're here after information." Carla was not stupid.

I didn't say anything.

"What do you really want to know?"

"I want to know if Lennie Senn arranged for you to accommodate the editor of the *Seattle Star*."

"John Anders?"

"Yes."

"I'll tell you all about it if you take me down the hall and treat me like whoever it is you love."

I thought about Shay. "I can't do that," I said.

"Oh, sure you can."

We paused for another song on the tape. Arlo Daw's groupies were laughing at another of his jokes. Their laughter was affected. The music started again.

"It won't be the same."

"I don't care. It's yes about Lennie and John Anders. I've been going there off and on for weeks. Anders didn't pay me though, Lennie did. The man who usually makes my arrangements is a cop named Louis Baird. Come on, let's go." She led me down the hall. There was laughter upstairs. I wondered who was up there.

Daw spotted me when we reappeared an hour later.

"Having a good time, Mr. Denson?"

"Never finer." I squeezed Carla's waist.

Daw grinned. I wondered how she restrained herself from kneeing him. Me too for that matter.

"There's somebody upstairs I'd like you and Mr. Sander to meet. He's free now also."

He turned. There was no question that I was to follow.

"No need to be embarrassed, you're not like him," Carla said as we trailed after him. Sander was waiting at the foot of the stairs with Helena, whom he treated like a borrowed Jaguar.

I smelled the pot before we got to the top of the stairs. The whole house was wired for sound. The tape now offered soft jazz. We stepped into a room where a naked girl was giving several men a private exhibition of anatomical stunts.

"Maybe more later," Daw said to the girl. She hopped up from the carpet and trotted out of the room.

A blond head with the hair cut fashionably just over the ears turned and the face froze in disbelief.

"What the fuck are they doing here?" Roy Hofstadter almost shouted at Councilman Daw.

Daw looked blank. "These are my friends, Roy. I believe you've met John Denson. This other gentleman is Bob Sander, also of the *Seattle Star*."

Hofstadter looked enraged.

Sander offered his hand but Hofstadter ignored him. Sander, who had done it to be outrageous, withdrew it with a wry look.

Daw laughed.

"I want to know what you're doing here?" Hofstadter asked me.

"I told you yesterday I was curious about the councilman's parties."

Although Daw had told Gilberto he didn't want anything in the newspapers, he really didn't mind. Everybody knew Daw was a crook who chased women. They knew about his parties. They didn't mind. As long as he did his job as councilman, what did it matter? The press had known about Wilbur Mills and his stripper long before he got drunk and drove into the tidal basin. Southern politicians don't mind a little rumor; they encourage it. The country boys expect a little chasing. If Wilbur had been absolutely proper, they would have thought he was either stupid or queer. But then the folks in Arkansas found out he hadn't been doing his job. Daw had no image to protect; he had no ambitions beyond fattening his wallet at the expense of the taxpayer.

With Roy Hofstadter it was different. He was the golden one. Local boy made good. Harvard Law. A charming smile. Sincere. Great on television. He would run for governor or senator with his wife and kids behind him on billboards.

He had for some reason trusted Arlo Daw. Now this.

"They're just here to have a little fun, same as you," Daw said.

"Great party," I said. "Carla and I are thinking about trying the tango later on."

"I think we've made Roy nervous," said Daw. "Maybe we shouldn't have interrupted the show. Shall we?" He motioned to the door with his hand. Sander and I and our girls followed him out. "Just a minute," he said. He opened a door down the hall and said something to someone inside.

The performer or whatever she called herself came back with him. Daw gave her an affectionate whack on her bare rump before she returned to her duties.

I doubted if Roy Hofstadter's heart was any longer in it.

"Girl needed a break anyway," Daw said. "That must be damn hard work, all that stretching. Gymnasts all have gorgeous bodies though, ever notice that?"

When he returned to the main floor, Daw was no longer interested in us. I had found some of what I wanted to know about Anders and Carla. The problem was that for each question I was able to answer, at least two more took its place. Questions were multiplying like gerbils.

Sander somewhat reluctantly parted with his loaned Jaguar. I said good-bye to Carla. I felt melancholy. So did she. She

130

would have been a marvelous person to have met at another place, another time.

She followed me to the door and gave me a soft kiss.

"Good-bye, John," she said.

"Good luck, Carla."

It was 4 A.M. when I finally got back to my apartment and to bed.

16

I SLEPT UNTIL 10 A.M., when I got up, ate a bowl of canned tomatoes, showered, cranked up the rented Fiesta, and headed in the direction of the *Star*. After six blocks I was sure nobody was following me. I pulled the Fiesta to the side of the road and hiked back to my apartment building. I slipped up the back way, eased down the hall, and very carefully tried the door to my apartment.

It was unlocked.

Roy Hofstadter didn't waste any time. A counterattack is worthless unless it's executed immediately. Hofstadter knew that. What he didn't know was that a worthy opponent anticipates. Or else he plain underestimated J. Denson, cauliflower eater and private gumshoe.

I thought momentarily of ringing my doorbell and letting Winston go through his act again. Winston was a stuffed English pit bull I bought at an auction in Baltimore. It wasn't just the fact that he was stuffed that made him so remarkable. It was the fact that he sat back on his haunches, muscles tense, fangs bared, ready to go for your jugular. He had malevolent, hateful eyes.

When you rang the doorbell, Winston went into his act. I had the doorbell wired to trigger a tape in Winston's innards so that he growled savagely until my visitors went away or I opened the door. Winston was easy to take care of. I didn't have to spring for dog food. All I had to do was dust him now and then to keep his coat shiny.

Inside, I knew, Hofstadter's people were having a bit of a time trying to find the right place to hide a bug amid the clutter of posters and memorabilia. I had plastic P-38's doing battle with Japanese Zeros and German Messerschmidts on the ceiling (the European theatre was in my living room; the battle in the Pacific took place in my kitchen). I had soccer pennants from the English First Division, a poster of a fabulous female butt, and a photograph of a man in a bowling shirt that featured a naked lady on a zebra. They had found a way to shut Winston up. Should I interrupt them or let them finish and tippy toe off in the crisp morning air?

I figured, why not let them plant their gear. If nothing else, I was interested in the current state of the art in electronic bugging equipment. The recorder would be voice-activated to thwart detectors. It would be a wee small thing. Fun to look for.

It would also be fun to think of Hofstadter having to re-trieve it from a pawn shop. I could leave it there with dirty limericks recorded on the tape or disc or whatever it contained.

There once was a man from Khartoum and et cetera.

When I got to the office I found out from Shay that Donalco no doubt referred to the Donald Alben Company, a Seattle firm that handled stocks and securities. Sander wasn't around. Powell had nabbed him for some newspaper work.

I drove back to my apartment and started looking for clever doodads. It wasn't hard. I found it on the underside of my favorite chair. Easy to install, just clamp it in place and punch the little button. It was about twice the size of a matchbox, battery-powered and voice-operated—which means it didn't run until there was noise in the room. I popped the top off it and found a miniature spool of what looked like fine copper wire. That would be the tape. Enough for weeks of recording, no doubt.

Hofstadter's men thought either they were awfully damned clever or I was awfully damned dumb. A combination of both, I suppose.

I pocketed the recorder and drove to a pawn shop on Pike called Hymie's. I knew Hymie from before when an insurance company hired me to try to find some stolen jewelry. Hymie had a sense of humor.

He squinted his eyes and giggled like a three-year-old when I told him what I had. He examined it eagerly and with not a little awe.

"By God, they really have the gear, don't they?" He slipped the lid off with his thumbnail and examined the spool with the bottom one-third of his trifocals. He shifted to the middle third and looked at me with a grin. "What do you propose?"

"That you give me fifty bucks for it and charge the cops a hundred to get it back."

Hymie punched open the cash register.

I drove back to the newspaper.

It was Saturday night: time for the Pig's.

"Would you like to accompany a gentleman to the Pig's tonight?" I asked Shay.

"The which?"

"Pig's Alley, down by Pike's. Class tavern."

"Who's the gentleman?"

I bowed low. Walt Raleigh at the curb.

Shay shrugged her shoulders. "Okay."

Rituals can be bad for your health. Never be predictable. But I didn't want to give up the Pig's. Some people can be predictable and get away with it. Take Rocky Marciano. He only knew how to do one thing: show 'em gloves, elbows, and the top of your head and keep on coming. It worked for him.

Me, I led with my chin.

Shay and I arrived at nine o'clock and were lucky to get a place to sit. The jazz trio was still playing: thick-fingered piano player, cornet player with the stiff handkerchief, and the whacked-out drummer. Loose, juiced, and heavy-lidded, they humped and screamed at lovers and demons. The bare boards shined. The sweat rolled. The music was sweet. Their plastic bucket had a few bucks. Not half damn bad.

I was about to sit down when I was run over by a Hell's Angels refugee. He was wearing engineer's boots run down at the heels, blue jeans with a hole that exposed a hairy cheek, and a T-shirt that said "Fuck me, Jack" on the front. He had a beard, greasy hair, wore a Gestapo officer's cap, and had a gold ring in one ear. His body odor was strong enough to knock a dog off a gut wagon. I wondered if he had picked my pocket on the crash.

He hadn't.

Shay seemed impressed. "You come here often?"

"Every Saturday night," I said. "Cary Grant and me."

I couldn't help but watch Hog Body with the Gestapo cap. He caught my eyes for the barest fraction of a second and looked away quickly.

Too quickly.

The jazz band had slowed to an erotic grind.

I considered Hog Body. "Shay, my love, would you like to dance?"

She brightened. "Then can we leave? This place gives me the creeps."

"On one condition."

"What's that?" She leaned across the table.

"You remember when you were seventeen years old and danced real slow with that stud with the muscles and the Clearasil on his zits?"

"Huh?" She looked puzzled.

"You danced real slow with your hands cupped under one another's buns."

"I never did that! That's disgusting."

"I want you to dance that way with me."

Shay looked puzzled. "You can fondle my buns all you want back at the apartment. Why do we have to do it in public?"

"Do you want me to spend the night in jail?"

"Huh?"

"Trust me for one dance."

She did.

"You have nice buns indeed," I said.

"You have hardly any at all. This is ridiculous."

I moved her so my back was to the band. "Try my left hip pocket with your left hand. Be casual."

She did. Good girl.

"What did you find?"

"A packet of something."

"Hold it by the edge and get the drummer's attention." The drummer had pupils as wide as the Holland Tunnel. "Tell him to be cool."

"Be cool," I heard Shay say over my shoulder.

I maneuvered my rear over the plastic bucket.

"Into the bucket."

"Done," she said. "On target."

I turned her around.

"Hey, glad you liked our music," said the drummer.

"Best you get that shit out of there fast," I said.

"Square," said the drummer.

I walked Shay back to the table, and before we got halfway there the cornet player went into a solo that was tough to believe. The drummer was spaced but not dumb.

No sooner had we sat down than a man with a gray herringbone jacket wearing thick-lensed glasses squatted by our table. He combed hair off his forehead with his fingers.

"No fuss, bub, but I'm a cop and you'll have to come along with me."

Shay looked wide-eyed.

I winked at her. "Give me a hug, Shay, and run on along. I'll be okay." I had her in my arms before the cop could say anything. I whispered in her ear: "Tell Charley Powell a vice captain named Baird had cocaine planted on me but I'm clear."

The cop had me by the arm.

I yanked it away. "I'll give you a call," I told Shay.

"Save it for your lawyer," the cop said. He grabbed me by the arm again.

The band had stopped playing. The merrymakers at the Pig's watched in silence.

"Hey Mr. Cornet Man, do you know 'Colonel Bogey's March'?" I yelled at the band.

The cornet player grinned. He was all teeth.

"Maestro!" I yelled. I yanked my arm a second time.

136

The cornet player adjusted the handkerchief around his instrument and gave me Colonel Bogey's. I gave my best impression of Alec Guinness marching proudly and confidently off to the sweatbox, a civilized officer and gentleman to the end. I marched grandly to the door, chest out, arrogant tilt to my chin.

I tell you the folks at the Pig's ate it up. The spaced-out drummer gave me a big pow! pow! pow! on the rim of his snares as I stepped out the door.

"You son of a bitch, you're going to pay for that," the cop said after we were outside. He led me to a squad car and pushed me roughly into the back seat. There was a detective waiting in the rear seat. Captain Louis Baird, still looking like an adolescent, sat up front.

The detective in the back with me slipped his hand into my left rear pocket.

"What did you find?" I asked.

"Where is it?"

"Where is what?" I turned my palms up in innocence.

Baird glared across the top of the seat. "You're a smart fucker. Make sure, Bill."

Bill tried just about everywhere he could think of.

"Get Jerry," said Baird.

The detective named Bill got out of the squad car and returned shortly with the detective who had led me out of the Pig's.

"It isn't on him," said Baird.

Jerry looked blank. "What do you mean it isn't on him? We never took our eyes off him."

"It isn't on him," confirmed Bill.

All three of them turned to me.

"I was once a real professional, gentlemen. One of Sam's boys. If your friend Hog Body in there is going to remain covert, there's one rule he's gonna have to remember. Never, but never, establish eye contact with a rabbit. Dumb rabbits, yes. Smart rabbits, no. Hog Body slipped that crap in my pocket, then couldn't restrain himself from a quick peek and a little gloat."

Baird shook his head. "Hog Body, that's good."

Jerry looked like he was ready to get violent. "What I want to know is what did you do with the stuff? You never touched your left hip."

I grinned.

"The blonde."

I shrugged my shoulders.

"That little bitch," said Jerry. He took defeat personally.

I ignored that. "Which reminds me," I said. "Hymie's."

Baird picked at his front teeth. "Hymie's?"

"The pawn shop on Pike. Just a few blocks up. I found a voice-operated recorder in my apartment. Dandy little thing. Those Japanese are clever bastards. Not much bigger than a matchbox. But what am I going to do with something like that?"

The detective named Bill started to grin. Jerry looked at Baird. Roy Hofstadter's brother-in-law looked like he'd sat on a fresh cow pie.

I opened my wallet and gave Baird the pawn ticket. "Hymie gave me fifty, says you can redeem it for a hundred."

Baird, who had seemed like a humorless bastard if there ever was one, then did something surprising. He started an outrageous guffaw. The poor man could hardly control himself. "Jesus Christ, wait till I tell Roy, he'll shit his fucking pants," he said.

His two detectives were snickering also.

"Get out of here, Denson, but don't think you can beat us three times running."

I got out of there fast. What he said was true: the odds were lousy.

I still couldn't resist having a little fun with Hog Body. I went back into Pig's Alley. When I opened the door the cornet player did a double take, dropped his tune, and struck up Colonel Bogey's once more.

I did a repeat performance with double the zest. The cops had lost a round; the folks at the Pig's cheered spontaneously. Hog Body, surrounded by bike nuts, cheered too. I aimed for his table. Those bikers find out he was an undercover cop, they would tear him apart. Poor Hog Body, he must have been on the verge of having a bowel movement when he saw me coming.

"Your blonde's gone but stick around, the beer's on me!" Hog Body bellowed. His eyes pleaded.

I paused to make him sweat a bit. In my business you can never tell when you might need a favor from a cop. "Hope you've got a fat wallet because I'm a trifle thirsty after those assholes."

Hog Body grinned. He dug at his behind.

I had my IOU.

17

I GOT RIGHT ON MY HOG BODY IOU the next morning I hated spending it so soon after I had it in the bank. Never was much for squirreling away nuts for the winter. I took a walk and found a pay phone to call Captain Gilberto. It was always possible that Roy Hofstadter was an old Green Bay Packer fan, he was of that age, and so knew from Bart Starr that if a play doesn't work once, it never hurts to come right back with it again.

One thing was certain: his troops wouldn't be so obvious the second time around. I didn't feel like spending the whole day ransacking my apartment for another electronic gadget.

It cost fifteen cents to make a local phone call in Seattle— a hateful bit of inflation. Ma Bell could stick that extra nickel in her ear as far as I was concerned.

If Captain James Gilberto had been a trifle reluctant to talk to me earlier, he couldn't have been more eager now. Word had gotten around about my stunt at the Pig's.

"Denson, you bastard, nice to know you're not in jail this morning." Gilberto started laughing and found it hard to stop.

"You guys are real fun people."

"Listen, you're a real hero down here. Stuck it up Baird's and broke it off. Too bad he wasn't inside to hear 'Colonel Bogey's March.' " Gilberto started laughing again. "And this morning, this morning, he . . ." Gilberto couldn't stop laughing. I was patient. "This morning he had to send a guy down to Hymie's to buy back his fancy little tape recorder. Hymie played dumb, pretended not to know it belonged to the cops. They had to pay him because they need his help in tracing fences."

"Listen, I want to get in touch with the undercover cop who planted the dope in my hip pocket."

There was a silence on Ma Bell's marvelous machine. "For Christ's sake, Denson, leave him alone. He was just doing his job. It took us two years to get him where he is."

I could see the Space Needle from my phone booth. "I don't want to get fancy with him or anything like that. I know he was doing his job. But he owes me, and I want to call the IOU."

Gilberto understood. "His name is Ron Steen, but after last night I'm sure it'll be Hog Body around here. I can't put you directly in touch with him; it would risk his cover. Give me a time and place and he'll be there."

"Bar called Andy's in the U district. Two hours from now, that'd be eleven A.M."

"He'll be there if it's possible. If he's not, you'll have to get back to me. We have to be careful."

"I understand," I said, and hung up.

I leaned a quarter against the curb, got the tire iron out of the trunk of the Fiesta, and gave the quarter a good whack. It bent nicely. Then I beat it on over to Andy's, which was open but deserted that time of day. A tall girl with a yellow blouse, stooped shoulders, and unblinking eyes sat on a padded stool behind the bar. She poured me a cup of coffee and went back to watching the traffic outside. It was a setup I'd cased earlier for future use. The jukebox was back in the corner and was flanked by one booth and the wall, not two booths.

I chose the booth between the jukebox and the wall. While the girl stared at people going places, I wired the booth for sound. I hid the tape recorder behind the jukebox and shoved

141

the bent quarter into the slot. A sign by the slot said not to use slugs, bent coins, or Canadian money. In red letters it said not to. Said it would jam the machine.

By eleven o'clock it was done. No sweat. I took a seat at the bar.

Hog Body was right on time. He was still in his biker's outfit. He no longer looked especially menacing but he still smelled like a toilet. The tall girl with the stooped shoulders regarded him as she might an orangutan eating feces at the zoo.

"We don't talk at the bar," he said.

"Pick a spot."

He picked the booth by the jukebox.

"Coffee?" I asked him.

"With cream," he said. He got up to play the jukebox.

"Two coffees, both with cream," I told the girl with the shoulders.

"This fucking machine won't take a quarter!"

"Somebody's been using slugs again. The sign's right there." The waitress brought us our coffee.

Hog Body didn't say anything. He looked nervously at the waitress, who was on her stool again, watching traffic.

"Listen," I said. "She doesn't give a damn what we talk about. She's just wishing a twenty-two-year-old chemistry major would walk in here, fall in love, and propose marriage so she could have a little affection, a couple of kids maybe, and a color television set."

That was true and Hog Body knew it. He had been working the sewers so long he was paranoid.

"I shouldn't be seen anywhere with you after last night. What do you want?"

"I saved your hide last night. Those bikers would've played soccer with your testicles."

"Ain't that the truth."

"Real fast now I want to know if there's an operation of high-class prostitutes working Seattle. I want to know if Vice Captain Baird is turning his head."

Hog Body took a sip of coffee. "Abadaba. Yes."

"Abadaba?"

"That's the name of the organization, Abadaba. Don't ask

me why, I don't know. Baird cuts the pie. I get a piece. So do those two detectives who were with Baird last night. You try to make waves, though, and somebody will cut you in half. That's not a threat from me; I'm just telling you the way Abadaba operates."

"Lennie Senn?"

"Head dude."

"Does Roy Hofstadter know about all this?"

Hog Body checked the waitress and thought a second before he answered. "Your IOU is just about up. Hofstadter is Baird's brother-in-law, but Baird is apparently on his own with Lennie Senn. What you have to keep in mind is that the public doesn't give a damn about wealthy guys screwing beautiful girls in fancy hotels. Let a hooker flash a thigh on Pike and that's another story. Let an Indian sail an empty whiskey bottle out onto the street and see what happens. Or maybe your publisher wants to make a few extra bucks with a series on junkies piling up in hospital emergency wards. See what happens then. We keep a handle on that shit and Hofstadter gets a public pat on the back." Hog Body was plainly nervous and wanted to get out of Andy's in the worst way.

I started to get up.

Hog Body looked wild-eyed. "You jam that machine?"

"No," I lied.

"You tape this conversation?"

"No," I lied again.

Hog Body got up too. "I think you might have. If you did and you use it, give me warning. I'm getting so I don't care anymore, but I don't want to be dead. Put it to the fuckers."

"I understand." I shook Hog Body's hand. He knew he had been taped. He didn't care. He wanted a shower.

18

IF HOG BODY WANTED a shower, I wanted a hell of a lot more. I wasn't sure just what. I had Haggart and his bank account, Fat Willie Fargo and his threat. I had Anders with his stocks and an apparent deal with Lennie Senn. I had Councilman Daw, Captain Baird, and the slick Mr. Hofstadter. All that no doubt fit together and made sense, but just how was beyond me.

There was just one player in the game who was yet to be scrutinized: Harold Balkin.

I slipped into a pay phone by a Texaco gas station and looked up Ruth Balkin Trotter. Finding her listed as Ruth Balkin, I knew what my opening move would be. I gave her number a try.

A rich woman's voice answered: "Yes?"

"My name is John Denson. I'd like to speak to Mrs. Trotter please."

"This is Ruth Balkin speaking."

A classic Denson opener. Offend the lady, then ask her for a favor. "Listen, I'm sorry. I always screw these things up. Seems like I don't know how to address a woman anymore."

Ruth Balkin laughed a good, strong laugh. "No problem, Mr. Denson, it's just that I'm not married to the guy any longer. No reason to lug his name around."

"Horses trot," I said.

"Precisely." She laughed again. "Just who are you, Mr. Denson, and what do you want?"

"I used to be an intelligence agent for Sam, then I was a reporter in Honolulu, then a private detective here in Seattle. Now I'm a reporter again for your paper. One of your boys. Are you with me?"

"I'm with you." Ruth Balkin laughed.

"So Wes Haggart was murdered and Charley Powell, knowing my background, detailed me to find the killer."

"Did you pass Charley's little test?"

"Wrote him a dandy," I said. "Leads I can do. It was the bullshit that got to me."

A car honked on the street behind me. "Where are you calling from, Mr. Denson?"

"A telephone booth by a Texaco station."

"Would you please tell me what I have to do with Wes Haggart's murder?"

"Probably nothing. But I can't go on assumptions or accept for a fact everything that's told me. People have a way of shading the truth in their favor. I want to talk to you about your stock in the *Star,* about your brother, Harold, and your opinion of John Anders. Charley tells me you were a solid reporter. You can't be dumb."

Ruth Balkin laughed. "That's very flattering. Can I say I agree without sounding arrogant?"

"I don't know why not. The thing I'd like to know right now is what I call you."

"Ruth."

"Well, Ruth, is there somewhere I can talk to you other than in a telephone booth?"

She laughed and gave me her address.

Ruth Balkin lived in a beautifully restored Victorian mansion on the north side of Seattle. It was a gorgeous, mad jumble of porticos, Gothic arches, gables, turrets, columns, shutters, garrets, you name it. The architect had apparently set out to demonstrate that he could duplicate the telling details of every classic period of architecture and what is more, friends, include them in one, yes, one single building. Did you see that, Mom?

I saw it and thought it was lovely.

So was its occupant.

Ruth Balkin was a sensual woman to whom age had been kind. Where she once might have been brittle and angular, she was now soft and mellow. There was a lovely fullness to her hips that was warm and comfortable. She had deep-set eyes that looked blue at first, then gray. She had smile lines around her mouth: she had seen the humor and been able to laugh along the way. For some odd reason her rich black hair was made even more handsome by an occasional strand of gray. It is said that women lose their youth and looks and have nothing. Something close to the reverse had apparently happened to Ruth Balkin. I wondered what it must be like to be curled up in a big warm bed with a woman like her.

"You were thinking, Mr. Denson?"

I was still standing there like a jerk after she had answered the door. "May I say something that is intended as a compliment and not as a con or a setup?"

"Certainly." She grinned.

"You have a nice, rich voice, solid and direct like those Linotypes you people replaced. Does that make any sense?"

Ruth Balkin sighed. "Yes, that makes sense, and I'm flattered. It's the nicest thing anybody has said to me in a long time. I'm sentimental too, incidentally. Won't you come in?"

I stepped in, first onto a polished hardwood floor, then onto a thick Oriental carpet. Her living room was furnished with gorgeous antiques. There were hanging baskets of houseplants everywhere. A large orange cat watched from a pillow on the carpet. The door closed behind me.

"I hope you didn't mean I'm worn out. They don't make Linotypes anymore; parts are almost impossible to get." She grinned.

"I can't imagine anyone wanting to replace your parts," I said. What I was thinking was that this was an exceptionally warm welcome. Ruth Balkin acted as though she knew me already. The suspicions she would normally have seemed somehow to be set aside, which told me I might not be getting everything I wanted. Had she talked to someone already? Who?

"Why thank you, Mr. Denson. Won't you sit down? Would you like a cold beer?"

I sat on an overstuffed sofa. The orange cat followed Ruth Balkin into the kitchen. "I'm thawing some liver for the cat," she called back. "The vet said to feed him liver. I chop it into little chunks and freeze it for him." She returned with two bottles of beer and two glasses on a tray. The cat didn't like it a damn bit that he hadn't got his liver, and he eyed me suspiciously. Was I to blame?

"Handsome cat," I said. Was I being set up?

She poured the beer. "He's a pain in the ass is what he is but I love him."

"Mmmmm," I said.

She brushed some cat fur from the blue slacks that handsomely packaged her rump, and sat opposite me in a high-backed soft chair. "Now then, what is it exactly you want to know and why?"

I had an idea she had been a reporter too long not to recognize a half-truth when she heard it. I told her everything that had happened to me to date, leaving out nothing except the details of bedding down Shay Harding.

"Well?" I said when I had finished.

"Well what?"

"Well, for starters, I guess, are you really pushed to the wall financially and are you easy pickings for Tobias Lane should the *Star* go into a slide?"

Ruth Balkin considered that for a moment, then regarded her bottle of beer, which was two-thirds empty. "First, how about another beer?" she said.

"Sold." I killed mine and gave her the empty. She went into the kitchen, followed by the orange cat.

"Thawed at last, thank God," she called back. The cat got his liver. He stayed for the gorge; she returned with our beer.

Ruth sat cross-legged in the soft chair, wiggled her toes in satisfaction, and regarded me for a moment. She might have been inspecting a Hereford bull at auction. I let her think and

147

looked at the gimcracks the cluttered her apartment: ceramic seagulls, soapstone seals and bears, dolls from various parts of the world. There were no fashionable aphorisms on little cards, no Sierra Club posters with quotes from Thoreau. Ruth Balkin's clutter was her own. She did her own thinking.

"Well, are you going to tell me?" I asked at last.

"I don't know why not. Have you ever known a liar, Mr. Denson? I'm talking about a liar, now, a real liar. Someone who could look you straight in the eye and rob you of your eyeteeth and you'd never know what happened."

I didn't know what to think of that. "What we're talking about is a Mickey Mantle of liars. A big-league liar."

"Yes," she said simply.

"Hell, I don't know." I shrugged my shoulders.

"My brother, Harold, is an accomplished, pathological, chronic liar. He lied to you on the *Papa's Ark*. He lied to you at The Gazebo."

I picked up a soapstone loon lying on top of a copy of *The Pickwick Papers* and ran my hand over its smooth, cool surface. "Where did you get this?" I said. "It's beautiful."

"In Victoria one afternoon. It was done by an Eskimo artist. You see the numbers scratched on the bottom. It's registered with the Canadian government."

"Tell me the lies. I like loons too; they have those lovely slender necks." I turned the loon again in my hand.

"It's yours. The loon is yours," she said.

I quickly put the loon back on Mr. Dickens's effort. "Hey listen, no, no," I said quickly.

"I'm an heiress, Mr. Denson. If I want another loon like that, I'll commission an Eskimo to carve it for me. This one is yours."

I left the loon on the book. "You were telling me about your brother's lies."

"My brother, Harold, is a wealthy man, Mr. Denson, but he always wanted more. He's tried for years to buy my share of the *Star*'s stock. I've always suspected he thought I should do as he told me because he was my older brother. Harold has never worked in the newspaper; he's never written or edited a story. He's never made a decision about the news. He likes it because of status and wealth. He likes it because he's on a first-name basis with governors and United States senators. He likes the parties and junkets; he likes the power." She stopped and picked at the little toe of her left foot.

"But he doesn't like newspapers?"

"He's never especially liked newspapers."

"What about your financial situation?"

She looked up from her toe. "I'm in some trouble, yes."

"And Tobias Lane?"

"The loathsome Mr. Lane has done his damndest to get my stock. He's tried for years. He's offered me handsome sums of money, so much that it's sometimes hard to believe. He knows I'll never sell to him because I hate what his chain does to newspapers. To him that's an ideological reason for not turning a profit, a stupid, possibly female reason." Ruth Balkin grinned at that one.

"Does your brother have any sort of option on your stock?"

"He has the right to match any other offer if I should ever decide to sell."

"What do you think he's up to? I mean, why should he lie to me? Why make it more complicated than it already is?"

"He probably thought you'd believe him, most people do. Did you, by the way?"

I poured myself some more beer. "I had my doubts; that's why I called you."

"What I think, Mr. Denson, is that if Wes Haggart was on the take it was a marvelous stroke of fortune for my brother. It couldn't come at a better time. I think he'd use whatever information you come up with to cripple the paper and force me to sell. I also think that within twenty-four hours he'd trade his *Star* stock for Lane stock at maybe triple the price and remain on as publisher with an enormous rather than just adequate fortune."

Had she talked to someone before me? Yes, I thought so. Was she telling the truth? I didn't know for sure. Whoever was telling the truth, there didn't seem to be any easy way out for the *Seattle Star*. I stood up and tugged at my belt. "Thank you for your help. I think I should be going now."

"Don't forget your loon, Mr. Denson."

I turned the loon slightly on the book. "If I get everything

149

straightened out and the *Star* remains in business as an independent newspaper, I'll take the loon as a commission, how's that?"

"Don't ever accept a gift you can't eat or drink, is that it, Mr. Denson?"

"The beer was good. The only way to operate. It should be the policy at the *Star* if it isn't already."

"It is and you're right. I apologize for offering it to you."

The cat returned from the kitchen. He leaned up against Ruth's leg and watched me leave with big yellow eyes that did not blink. Ruth Balkin shielded her eyes from the sun with her left hand. The sun brought out the shine of her hair. I squatted on my haunches and pulled some grass from the lawn. It was beginning to cloud but the sun still held forth in a patch of blue. Ruth Balkin stroked the cat's back. The cat arched its back to receive her hand and looked to the heavens with a look of sublime bliss.

I envied the cat. I said good-bye to Ms. Balkin and drove back to the *Star,* where Shay waited, going through notes for a story.

"Well, Mr. Detective?" she said.

"Talked to the publisher's sister. Nowhere."

"Nowhere?"

"Well, she confirmed she's in financial trouble. She said brother Harold has never really given a damn about newspapers, which doesn't surprise me. And she said, yes, Tobias Lane has been after her stock."

Shay grinned. "Why don't you ask Tobias about that?"

"Ask Tobias?"

"Sure, he's been here in Seattle for the last ten days nagging Ms. Balkin about her stock. He gave her a standing offer to triple the market price of her *Star* shares."

"Triple? How did you find that out?"

She shrugged. "Ms. Balkin."

"Ms. Balkin?"

"I talked to her yesterday. Tobias Lane told her if she could get her hands on Harold's shares, the offer's good for those too. He said he'd guarantee her Harold's job as publisher on top of that. Tenure guaranteed. What do you think of them apples, Mr. Denson?"

"Shit." I slumped in my chair. "Why didn't she tell me?"

"We had a nice chat yesterday, Ruth Balkin and I. I told her I liked you a lot but think you have a small sexist streak in you."

"Oh," I said. "What do I do now?"

Shay laughed. "Well, I'd pick up the phone like a man and give her a call. Tobias Lane is staying in the Evergreen Penthouse; maybe she can help you get to him."

I gave Ruth Balkin a call with Shay watching me, giggling. "Say, this is John Denson again, I was wondering if maybe you could give me some help in talking to Tobias Lane." I could hear classical music in the background.

"Been talking to Shay, huh?"

"Uh-huh."

"Tobias Lane doesn't like to talk to newspaper reporters, much less detectives, but if you hustle on back here maybe I can help you out."

"I'm on my way."

"Find out what you want?" Shay asked after I had hung up.

"You'd make a good gumshoe yourself."

"I do my best," she said.

The cloud bank had slipped in front of the sun by the time I got back to Ruth Balkin's house, and it was suddenly chilly. She was waiting for me on the porch. I could hear the rain rattling leaves in the distance as it swept toward us over the city. I leaned against the doorjamb and waited for Ruth to take the lead.

"I think I should call him and tell him a reporter named John Denson paid a visit asking questions about my stock and Tobias Lane. I should tell him a divorced friend of mine once hired this very same John Denson to investigate her husband's philandering. I should tell him you were chasing a rumor that Wes Haggart was on the take before he was murdered."

"Not bad," I said.

She held up a hand. "That isn't all. I'll tell him Wes Haggart was an honorable man and anybody who says he was on the

151

take is full of it. I'll tell him he can take his private detective and shove him: I'm still not selling."

Ruth Balkin went back inside and I followed.

"There's more beer in the refrigerator if you'd like another while I call."

I did as she said and sank into another soft chair, beer in hand, while she made the call. She was gorgeous: righteously indignant at first, damned near screaming at the end.

I had two more beers and listened to soft jazz on Ruth Balkin's fancy machine before I tried my hand at calling Tobias Lane. A woman with a voice out of a wet dream answered the phone.

"Yes?" she said.

"My name is John Denson. I'm a reporter for the *Seattle Star*. I'd like to arrange an appointment to interview Mr. Lane."

There was a slight pause. "Mr. Lane doesn't grant interviews to the press."

I liked the way she had said "grant." "Would you ask anyway? Tell him the name is Denson."

"I'll try, honey, but I'll tell you in advance it won't do any good."

"Try, that's all I ask."

"It'll be a minute," she said.

I waited. It was something short of a minute when a man answered the phone. "This is Tobias Lane, Mr. Denson. Did my secretary tell you I don't grant interviews to the press? I don't trust reporters."

"That's what she said, but I figured nothing ventured, nothing gained. I'm a good writer, not a shark. I don't interview someone with my mind already made up."

Tobias Lane laughed at that. "Well, hell, that's what bloody rules are for, made to be broken, eh, Mr. Denson?"

"That's what they say."

"One thing though, how was it you got my number, Mr. Denson?"

I cleared my throat. "Well, the truth is I interviewed Ruth Balkin about a half an hour ago. She became enraged and claimed I was your employee. I denied that, of course, and she accused me of being your pimp. An odd woman, Ms. Balkin.

Once I knew you were staying in the Evergreen, finding your telephone number was a piece of cake."

"You've been in the business awhile, I see."

"A while."

Tobias Lane laughed again. "What the hell, come on up. If I don't like your questions, I simply won't answer them. That sound fair?"

"As far as I'm concerned. I'll see you in a few minutes, Mr. Lane." I hung up.

Ruth Balkin looked like she'd been holding her breath the entire conversation.

"I'm not sure we should have told him about the Wes Haggart bit, but I don't think he would have talked to me otherwise," I said.

"Do you think Wes Haggart was a Harry?" she asked.

"I don't know. If Tobias Lane knows the possibility, I'm certain he doesn't know for sure either. Until he knows for sure there's nothing he can do but wonder like the rest of us."

I shook Ruth Balkin's warm, soft hand and headed for Tobias Lane's penthouse—the highest and fanciest in all of Seattle.

19

THE GIRL WHO ANSWERED the doorbell wore an inadequate halter and a pair of trousers that rode low on her hips.

"My name is John Denson. Mr. Lane should be expecting me."

"Of course, Mr. Denson. If you'll just wait here for a second." She had dimples on the flat of her back just above her rump.

She was replaced almost immediately by Tobias Lane, Fleet Street manipulator, owner of an international chain of newspapers, multimillionaire, son of a British colonial official in the West Indies and Leslie Holt, daughter of Geoffrey Holt, former British Chancellor of the Exchequer.

Tobias Lane had been around too many ass kissers and yes-man in his day. A little brass was in order. "Mr. Tits and Ass himself," I said, and we shook hands.

Tobias Lane brightened. "Boobs and bums, Mr. Denson."

"Tits and ass. Boobs and bums. They both sell newspapers."

Lane grinned. "Indeed they do. I saw your glazed eyes as I came in. My secretary's bums, I assume."

"I like those dimples back there. Always have."

"So do I, as a matter of fact. Find them damned erotic."

Tobias Lane was a small man, perhaps five foot five and maybe 120 or 130 pounds. He wore white shoes and sleek white slacks. He had a slight paunch. Gray hair from his chest showed at the open neck of a mint green shirt. He had a high forehead, a handsomely styled mane of gray hair, and small brown eyes overwhelmed by large black pouches. He wasn't especially pretty but he was rich, smart, and successful. If he wanted something, he bought it. He watched me now, calculaing my price.

I would have told him that cauliflower goes for four bits a head in the summertime but he wouldn't have believed me. Nobody sells out for raw cauliflower.

"Would you like a drink, Mr. Denson?" Without waiting for me to answer, he stepped through an open door to what I assumed would be his bar. It was. A handsome thing. The view through a large window was of the city lights and the Sound. The Space Needle was on our right; the city and its hills were spread out below us in a vast, impressive panorama. "What'll it be?"

I held up my left hand and winked. "When I buy, Mr. Lane, screw-top red, when a man who owns eighty-seven daily newspapers buys, I drink Wild Turkey bourbon with just a tad bit of water."

Lane grinned.

I took the drink and gave it a sip. "Good whiskey. My old man got thrown in jail for making rye nowhere near as good."

Lane smiled, poured himself some as well, and looked out the window. "Lovely city, Seattle."

"Yes it is." I was wondering where to begin. How do you go about asking Tobias Lane if he was trying to rip off another independent newspaper?

He saved me the trouble. "Mr. Denson, I don't give interviews to newspaper reporters. They rarely get a story straight. They regard me as Lucifer himself. But you know and I know I'm just out to make a few bucks."

I shrugged my shoulders.

"But I can't be quoted like that in a newspaper, can I? I agreed to talk to you because I know you're investigating a

155

suspicion that the late Mr. Haggart was an extortion artist. I'm curious."

I cleared my throat.

"You're wondering how I knew that?"

"You could say that." I watched him over the rim of my whiskey glass.

"I'm not sure telling you would serve any useful purpose. Suffice it to say I know. As I say, I'm curious."

"What would be the point of telling you?"

"Money?" He raised his eyebrows and cocked his head slightly.

"No." I shook my head.

"Well, as to the usual question, of course I'm trying to gain controlling interest in the *Star*. I've been trying to do that for years; everybody knows that. You hardly had to interview me to find that out. Help yourself to some more whiskey. You know where the ice is."

I helped myself. "If Wes was on the take, would the damage deliver the *Star* into your hands?"

"That Balkin woman is obstinate as hell. But she'll come around. Everybody has his price. Yes, if Wes Haggart did that, I'll own controlling interest in the *Star* in six months."

"How about Harold Balkin?"

"What about him?"

"Is he vulnerable too?"

Lane shook his head and ran his fingers through his mane of gray hair. "Harold Balkin doesn't have to sell if he doesn't want to."

I dumped a couple more ice cubes into my whiskey. "But you yourself just said everybody has his price."

Lane grinned. "Yes, I did, didn't I? I'm sure Harold has his as well."

"If I can eat it or drink it, I'll take it. Beyond that, no."

"A curious code. Where did you come by that, the movies?" He was genuinely interested.

I helped myself to some more of his whiskey. I was in for a session of the spins when I went to bed and a headache in the middle of the night, but I didn't care. I thought about his question. "When I was a kid, I drove a truck in wheat harvest.

I made four, maybe five trips to the elevator in a twelve-hour shift. Wheat, as far as the eye can see." I waved my arm expansively and looked out over the city of Seattle. "And heat, little twisters leaping and dancing in the distance. The temperature a hundred and eight, maybe a hundred and ten in the shade, only there isn't any shade, Mr. Lane. Me, I'm sixteen years old and driving a five-speed, four-wheel-drive truck, straight out of Big War II. You double-clutch that sucker and tap the accelerator with each shift. What do you suppose I did in all that heat?"

I wasn't sure what Lane's role was in the Wes Haggart mystery. I had no reason to like him especially, but Lane was a player and not a bullshitter, and for that reason at least, I respected him.

"You thought about sex." He laughed.

"Yes, that's one thing." I watched him over my glass.

"And the other?"

"I read paperback books. The hired man kept two enormous cardboard boxes filled with westerns and mysteries. Simple reading, good guys and bad; I knocked off four, maybe five a day. Crapped up my mind."

"So you determined to become a Lancelot of sorts." Tobias Lane giggled.

That wasn't bad. I had to laugh too. "Something like that."

"Would you like to be an editor on one of my papers?"

"You're not drunk enough for that kind of bullshit."

"You don't like my kind of journalism, Mr. Denson?"

I shrugged. "People gotta laugh. People gotta cry. People gotta know what's going on in the world."

"You didn't answer my question."

"I once saw a picture of a fat man on a bar stool in one of your papers at a grocery store check-out stand. It was marvelous."

Tobias Lane looked surprised. "I think you can be a bit more honest than that. You've already gotten everything you're going to get from me."

"I guess I like to read stories about venereal disease among wild donkeys as much as the next guy."

Lane took a step back and looked hurt. "People want to be

thrilled. They're more interested in big-boobed actresses than foreign policy. They want to read about donkeys; their taste is ours."

"I rest my case with H. L. Mencken." Mencken, who wrote for the *Baltimore Sun* in the 1920's, had a quote for every occasion. He was my favorite.

Lane leaned forward a touch. "How's that?"

"He said nobody in this country has ever gone broke underestimating the intelligence of the public."

Lane grinned. "I do own several of what you would call 'good' newspapers. They're high-minded but boring. Nobody really reads them, so they never make any money. I support them with the trash you despise, Mr. Denson. They're an expensive hobby for me, like electric trains. Besides, they're my key to the nicer clubs." He winked.

"Better they're subsidized by boobs and bums than by the government."

He shrugged. "My offer to you still stands. It's good now, a year from now, or five years from now."

"You'd can me in a year."

"Possibly," said Tobias Lane. "But keep up the old pecker, Mr. Denson." That was his signal that it was time for me to go. His attempt at a bribe had failed.

I shook his hand and left. The girl with the dimples failed to make an appearance when I left. I was disappointed.

20

I HAD BARELY GOTTEN THE FIESTA in fourth gear when a blue light began flashing in my rearview mirror. I pulled obediently to the side of the road and waited. I rolled down the window. It was Louis Baird's sidekick, Bill the detective.

"You," he pointed his finger at me, "come with me." He pointed at the squad car.

I went with him.

Roy Hofstadter was sitting in the back seat. I slid in beside him, and Bill the detective took us for a drive.

Hofstadter said nothing for several minutes, and we watched gas stations, used-car dealers, fried-chicken carry-out, taverns, and pizza joints.

"I like rides," I said. "Why don't we go down to First Avenue? We could look at the drunks and whores. We could maybe have a beer at the Pig's and talk over old times. Stuff like that."

Hofstadter looked at me mildly. "Why were you talking to Tobias Lane?"

"Boy, you'd make a real editor. Tobias Lane owns the second largest newspaper chain in the world. He's copy."

Hofstadter shook his head. "Tobias Lane doesn't give interviews to the press. He knows what a bunch of penny-ante assholes reporters are."

"Never let the truth stand in the way of a good story; that's always been my motto."

"Only you aren't a reporter anymore, are you, Mr. Denson? You're a private hired by the *Seattle Star* for reasons I find curious."

I fumbled my wallet out my hip pocket and gave him my press card. "See there: John Denson, reporter."

"Put it back."

I put it back. We were at a stop sign and three young thugs crossed the street in front of us, backfields in motion. The light turned and Bill sat, still staring.

"It's turned, Bill," said Hofstadter.

"What?" Bill was momentarily confused.

"The light. The light turned."

"Oh."

We were off again.

Hofstadter returned to me. "You're trying to find out whether Wes Haggart was on the take, and Tobias Lane was naturally curious, he being in the market for newspapers and all."

I gave him what can only be described as an oddball giggle. "Fat Willie doesn't waste time, does he?"

Hofstadter tried not to look disappointed.

"He tried to peddle us that line too, but we aren't buying," I said. "You can run with it if you want. The line is that he covered an arson case involving a wholesale food warehouse. Only he didn't have anything to do with it. Your cops did."

"North, please, Bill." Hofstadter took a deep breath. "You're sure about that one?"

"Got it from a cop."

"I'm hungry. You like chicken, Denson?"

"Sure."

We pulled over to a Colonel Sanders' and Bill the detective bought us Cokes and a cardboard bucket of chicken.

"I like breasts," Hofstadter said.

"That little gal at Arlo Daw's do stunts with her boobs?"

Hofstadter didn't like that. He looked quickly at Bill, then back at me.

"I like thighs myself," I said. "You owe me one from Arlo's party, old bucko."

Hofstadter chewed on his deep-fried breast and considered his next move. Bill drove and ate a wing.

"So what did Tobias Lane want with you? He doesn't give a damn who murdered Wes Haggart."

"Tobias Lane's too smart to go off half-cocked on a rumor spread by a two-bit jerk like Fat Willie."

Hofstadter wiped his mouth off with a paper napkin and went for another piece of chicken of no recognizable shape. "And Mrs. Trotter, why did you talk to her?"

"Wes Haggart's murderer."

"How could she help?"

"She goes by Balkin again now that she's divorced. She used to work with Wes on the *Star*. I was after rumor, unsettled scores, gossip, that kind of thing. Collect enough bits and pieces and you never know."

Hofstadter rapped on the Plexiglas shield that separated us from the front seat. Bill the detective made an illegal U-turn and we started back. When we got to the Fiesta I motioned for Hofstadter to follow me.

"You wait," he told Bill, and came with me.

I paused between the squad car and my Fiesta. "I deliver the murderer to you with credit, you work a deal?"

Hofstadter looked up at the stars. "You don't like tape recorders, do you? It depends, Denson."

"I guarantee it won't be anything you can't live with. I'll throw in the business at Arlo Daw's house as a bonus."

"We'll see," he said. He returned to the squad car and was gone.

Fat Willie had been to Hofstadter. There wasn't much doubt of that. Only Willie didn't tell him about the $5,000 deposits in Wes Haggart's checking account. Roy Hofstadter had found that little tidbit on his own: an exquisite, secret pearl to contemplate. He was sitting in the back of that squad car right now feeling grand, thinking he had finessed me, a jerk who had the nerve to talk deals.

I hustled on down to the *Star* building the first thing next morning. I wanted to talk to a fiftyish lady named Altoona Maas. The Altoona was after the town in Pennsylvania where she was born. Lucky she wasn't born in Blue Ball or Bird in Hand—Pennsylvania has some marvelous little towns. Altoona, so I was told, was a by-the-books payroll clerk.

She wore large eyeglasses then fashionable among feminists but her gray hair was tinted pale blue, a practice indulged in by wealthy matrons who donate to art museums. Altoona spoke in a rich baritone. If I hadn't known better, I'd have thought she was Lyndon Johnson in drag. Golda Meir with blue hair.

"May I help you?"

"Yes, my name is John Denson. I'm new city-side and I've been detailed by Charley Powell to find Wes Haggart's murderer. I would like to look at his payroll cards, please."

"I know who you are. I processed your payroll data. The answer is no."

I wanted to take her by the blue hair and shake her, but I remained calm, gave her a grin, and tried my boyish charm routine. "Oh sure, I realize the company has a policy about that kind of thing, but since Wes is dead, Charley said it'd be okay."

Altoona looked at me coldly. "No."

"Charley said it'd be okay."

"I don't care what Charles Powell thinks, does, or says. He runs the city room. I run payroll. The rules say no so the answer is no, Mr. Denson."

"I'm trying to find out who murdered one of our reporters."

"I'm sure the police are capable of doing that, Mr. Denson. A rule is a rule."

"Would you mind phoning Charley Powell?"

"Yes, I would mind. According to the *Star*'s organizational chart, the city room is parallel to and not superior to payroll."

I leaned over the edge of her tidy desk. "Then how about John Anders?"

That made her pause slightly. "Mr. Anders, the editor?"

"That's the only Anders I know around here."

"Mr. Anders has much more important things to do than

162

indulge your whims, Mr. Denson. You'll learn that when you've been here long enough." Altoona Maas did not like to issue a surly edict and then have to back off.

I picked up the receiver of her telephone and punched the switchboard operator. "Could you get me John Anders's office, please?" There was an efficient click and Anders's new secretary answered. "I'd like to speak to Mr. Anders, please. Tell him John Denson is on the line and it's very important."

A moment later I had Anders on the line while Altoona watched, hating me.

"I'm in the office of a lady named Altoona, your payroll clerk. Will you please instruct her to let me see Haggart's records and, while you're at it, tell her to answer any other questions I might have."

Anders laughed. "Jesus, she's a sweetheart, isn't she? Hard as nails and the rules are her religion, but she does a job. Put her on the line."

I handed Altoona the receiver and she listened, saying nothing. When Anders was finished she thanked him, hung up, and looked at me as coldly as before.

"Now then, what can I do to help you, Mr. Denson?"

"I'm glad you follow the book, ma'am. It's good to know my records are my private business."

Altoona Maas didn't flatter. "As I said, what would you like to know?"

"Has anybody besides me examined the records or asked to examine them?"

"A police detective came here. He wanted to know how much Wes made each month and what his deductions were, but he didn't look at the records. I did. Legitimate police inquiries are allowed by *Star* policy."

"I see. Who besides you has access to this room and the payroll records?"

Altoona looked surprised. "Why no one, Mr. Denson. I'm surprised you asked that question."

"By no one you mean absolutely no one, not even janitors or the publisher?"

"The janitors are an unfortunate exception, but the cabinets are always locked. As to the publisher, I'm sure Mr. Balkin has a key to every lock in the building; it's his newspaper, after all."

I nodded my head sympathetically. "Has Mr. Balkin ever asked to see Wes Haggart's payroll records or phoned for information on them?"

To a committed follower like Altoona Maas, such a question was outrageous. She cleared her throat by way of a stall. "No," she said at last. She was covered by Anders's instructions.

"Thank you. I'd like to see the main card listing Haggart's payroll data. I'd like you to handle the card by the edges and lay it on your desk for me to see."

Altoona did as she was told, exactly. I took the information boxes one at a time, beginning with name, last, middle initial, first. "Wes had his money sent automatically to his checking account each month, is that right?"

"That's correct."

"And this is his checking account number, is that also right?"

"Yes, it is."

"I want to take this card for a couple of days. You may call Mr. Anders if you like and get his okay."

Altoona called Anders. He gave his okay.

"I want you to tell no one, absolutely no one, that I took this card, do you understand? If Anders calls back, you can tell him, but no one else. No one."

"No one. Done," she said.

I left the lady named Altoona with Wes Haggart's payroll card in an envelope. I didn't want to smudge the prints.

21

CHARLEY POWELL SAT ALONE in a city room that was empty except for his memories, the newly installed VDTs, Shay, a bearded labor reporter in a fedora, and a six-foot-three-inch woman who covered the city's schools. Charley was staring at a Styrofoam cup full of coffee when I pushed my way through the glass door. Shay watched me enter, and I could tell from the look in her eyes something was wrong.

"Hey, what's the matter, Shay?" I called.

Shay blinked once, twice, but said nothing.

"Charley?"

Powell looked up from his cup of coffee. His mouth fell slightly open as though he were in a stupor and he ran his left hand along his chin. He started to speak but thought better of it and closed his mouth.

"Hey, Charley!"

He took a sip of coffee.

"What's the matter, Charley?"

"Ask Shay," he said softly.

I turned to Shay. "Well?"

"I'm going to Los Angeles, John," she said.

I sat down. "Oh?"

"You remember the producer I interviewed the other day, the one with the girls? Well, he called yesterday and offered me a job as a television reporter for the ABC-TV affiliate in Los Angeles at nearly double my salary here."

It's a cliché, I know, but it's true: there are times when a person doesn't know whether to laugh or cry. For me this was one of them.

I turned to Charley Powell of the gray eyes with black pouches. "For Christ's sake, tell her, Charley!"

Powell shrugged. "I told her, John. You tell her."

"I've heard it. I know, I know," said Shay.

If Charley had failed, I knew I wouldn't do much better. Shay had been touched by the American dream. But I had to try. "Do you know what the *Star* pays you for, Shay?"

"I don't want to hear," she said. She avoided my eyes.

"For your brains. You're a professional. You do a job. The readers don't know what you look like; they don't know whether you have three breasts or are eight feet tall. You know what that producer wants with you."

"You've had your turn, why shouldn't he?" Shay snapped. First Charley Powell, now me. She'd had enough lectures.

I didn't stop. "That's not what I mean and you know it. Those people on the tube aren't journalists, they're actors and actresses. It's show business, Shay, and when the ratings are uncertain they don't blame it on the news, they look at the bodies who read it."

"I've heard all that, John."

"Look, this is a city of a million and a half people. Some hoods try to rub out a nobody named Denson for snooping around their sex shops. Think about this: there is about twenty minutes of news in a half-hour program after you subtract the time for the ads. Those guys spent about five minutes—one-fourth of their news time—showing close-ups of a blanket I had bled on. You call that news?"

"I know all that, John."

"The network people give us an almost unrelieved diet of shootings in Belfast, kidnappings in Rome, and skirmishes in Beirut with an oversimplified report by an economics reporter

166

thrown in to justify it as news. It's show business, Shay, no place for anybody with brains."

"I know, I know."

"And you, one day they'll conclude that you're not what they wanted after all, that male viewers don't entertain fantasies about you, that you're shy in the boobs, thin in the rump, long in the nose, and that'll be it. Your brain won't enter into it. You can have acorns up there for all they care."

Charley Powell got up without a word and walked off in the direction of the men's room. He had a lot on his mind.

Shay leaned toward me. "I have to give it a try, John," she said evenly. "I have to see what it's like. What future do I have here? Charley'll be nursing his dream that people really give a damn. You'll return to your detective fantasy. You know, I really believed John Anders was fighting for the right to publish those ads out of principle, because he believed in a free press. I admired him. He was fighting my fight, our fight. And what did we find out? Lennie Senn. You want me to stay. A profession that matters. You tell me that, John; you tell me that when our publisher is locked up at Walla Walla with our photographer taking his picture as they take him through the gates."

"Balkin in Walla Walla?"

She looked me in the eye. "That's his name last time I knew. I can add too, Mr. Detective. Well, I talked to his sister too. I talked to Altoona on the same hunch you had. I know the real Harry is Harold Balkin. I just can't prove it. I don't especially want to. I'm getting out, that's all. You finish it."

"You knew I talked to Altoona?"

"Sure, I knew that. She called me five minutes after you walked out the door. Altoona's a friend of mine. She may be a hard-bitten old gal, but she likes to have a drink with the girls."

Powell was on his way back from the toilet. "Do me a favor will you, Shay? Don't mention this to Charley until I get everything checked out."

"If the Harry isn't Wes, it's Harold." She shook her head sadly. "I won't say anything."

I tilted my chair back on its rear legs and looked at Charley

167

Powell. "I think we've lost her, Charley." I couldn't believe it; Shay was right with me all the time. Well, yes I could too believe it. The question now was whether we were right. Was Harold Balkin really the Harry?

"Yes, but we'll still fight the good fight, won't we, Denson?"

"Yes, we'll give it a go." Shay was beginning to cry. I put my arm around her. "And Charley, if in a year from now the high roller decides she is in fact a trifle thin in the rear, will you have her back?"

"We always have room on the *Star* for brains, Shay."

But she wouldn't return. I knew that. Charley Powell knew it. Shay knew it. The camera does something to them. They're never the same afterward. They can't go back. They see themselves there on the set and they can't return to a typewriter. Could I really blame her? If the offer had been made to me, would I have turned it down?

I got up, stunned at my loss of Shay, and left the city room without looking back. The hurt would disappear after a time. But Charley Powell was right: the shits could kill us but we shouldn't give up.

22

I TOOK A STROLL through the *Star*'s parking lot to see if there was something I could steal from Harold Balkin's silver Mercedes. There wasn't. He kept it locked. I considered the rearview mirror but thought better of it: someone might think it a bit strange to see a man with a screwdriver removing the rearview mirror from the publisher's Mercedes. Well, there's always a way. I retreated to the building, found the publisher's office number on the big board in the lobby, and took an elevator.

Harold Balkin's secretary wasn't in. Gossiping in the coffee shop, no doubt.

Good old Harold wasn't in either. Such luck.

And his door was unlocked. The gods were smiling on John Denson. I walked on in and helped myself to the hand-blown paperweight on his desk. Handsome thing. I walked out with nobody being the wiser. Just like downtown!

Loaded thus with Wes Haggart's payroll card and Harold Balkin's hand-blown paperweight, I drove my rented Fiesta to Captain Gilberto's office.

Even he was in. Every once in a while you have one of

those days where you meet the ball square on with the fat of the bat.

But when Gilberto narrowed his left eye slightly I began to wonder if this was really my time at the plate.

"We've been hearing stories about you, Denson."

"Oh, yeah?" I laid Balkin's paperweight and Haggart's payroll card on his desk, careful to handle the card by the edges.

"I think I need you in here like a hole in the head. I hear stories about you and Arlo Daw, stories about you and Louis Baird, stories about you and Roy Hofstadter."

"Let me see now." I tapped my chin with my forefinger. "I saw Hofstadter and a performing girl at Arlo Daw's and after that his brother-in-law tried to plant dope on me at Pig's Alley. Then just last night Roy himself became terribly curious as to why I interviewed a man named Lane, staying in a penthouse with a girl with a tremendous rump, dimples right here." I massaged the small of my back.

Gilberto closed his eyes and shook his head. "Denson, Denson, I know all that. Cops gossip worse than women at a beauty salon. The thing of it is, do I really need you here in my office? If Hofstadter should ever find out I set you up for Daw's party, it's my ass."

I waved him quiet with my hands. "Shush, shush, I'm the very epitome of discretion. Is that the word, epitome?"

"You could say 'soul of discretion' if you go for clichés."

"Clichés are fine by me; after all, I'm a private detective."

Gilberto grinned. "Okay, now what is this crap?" He motioned to the card and the paperweight on his desk.

"The card is Wes Haggart's payroll card. I swiped the paperweight from someone's desk."

"Oh, I see. Whose desk, exactly?"

"I swore I wouldn't tell."

"Who? Who did you make this promise to?"

"Me. I promised myself I wouldn't tell."

"That makes sense. And what do you want me to do with them?"

"I want you to buck them over to your lab and find out if there are any prints on the card that match the prints on the paperweight."

170

Gilberto rested his forehead in the palms of his hands. "Do you have any idea how complicated it is to get those guys to do anything, even legit police business?"

"I assume you have to fill out forms with a case number, detective in charge, date, place and time the objects were collected, under whose authority, with the proper initials, in triplicate, et cetera, et cetera."

"That's it, bucko."

"Can't you just bullshit them a little? Don't you give them a fifth or something at Christmastime?"

"Those guys are serious, Denson. They never joke; they never laugh; they never do things for the hell of it."

"What if I was to steal a form, fill it in, and simply walk in and hand it to them?"

Gilberto brightened. "And how would you sign it?"

"A. C. Doyle."

"Bullshit."

"They never really read those things; this'll prove it." That appealed to Gilberto's sense of humor. He gave me a request form and helped me fill it out. He also helped me with the cop lingo necessary for the form printed on the outside of the evidence envelope.

"One more thing, Denson."

"What's that?"

"One more thing, then we're quits as far as IOUs and my daughter are concerned."

I hated to give up on a good thing, but I had worked Gilberto for all he was worth. "As far as I'm concerned we were even up long ago, Captain."

"You didn't hear this from me."

I looked shocked. "My heavens, no!"

"I got this by rumor so it can't be traced anyway. They found the weapon that killed Wes Haggart and the two girls. It was found on the body of a gent named Bill Morton who was on parole from the penitentiary, where he had spent two years on an armed robbery rap."

"On the body?"

"Bill Morton was murdered in a sleazy hotel on First Avenue."

171

"How come I haven't heard about this?"

Gilberto grinned. "Word has it that Hofstadter wants to keep it on ice for a few days. He is especially concerned that you newspaper people don't find out."

"Why are you telling me?"

"We cops like prosecutors who look after cops, not themselves."

I took the form to the police lab. There were two men in the lab, playing cards. One was obese, needing two chairs really, one for each buttock. But he made do with one so as not to appear too outlandish. His companion, of ordinary size, stroked his red beard and declined to look up from his cards when I entered.

"Yes?" asked the fat man.

"We have to have a print check."

"Oh?" The fat man laid down his cards. The man with the red beard looked at me, annoyed.

I handed the fat man the card. He studied it. The man with the red beard snatched it from his hands before he had finished.

"Just who in the hell is this A. C. Doyle?" Red Beard demanded.

"Arthur Conan Doyle," I said.

"Get smart with me and you won't get your prints."

"We call him Al," I said. "His real name is Alfred Clyde Doyle."

"We can have this for you tomorrow."

I shook my head. "Now."

"What do you mean 'now'?"

"Look at the card. It'll only take you a few minutes. I'll play your hand if you want."

Red Beard reread the order form. "Give me the envelope," he said.

I gave him the envelope. He disappeared into another room where he kept his paraphernalia, like some mad alchemist. The fat man didn't move, didn't say anything. We waited.

Red Beard came back in five minutes. "We've got matching prints on the card and the paperweight. It'll take a few minutes to run the prints through the computer for an ID."

"That's okay, it's not necessary in this case."

The fat man looked up. Red Beard looked suspicious. "It's always necessary. The computer run is S.O.P."

"Did you put the stuff back in the envelope?"

"Yes," he said. "The data's taped to the front there."

I snatched it from his hand and calmly walked out the door. Red Beard didn't know what to do so he did nothing. The fun would start when he sent a report to a Captain A. C. Doyle complaining about a lackey who ran off with the evidence before he could run the data through the computer.

Someone would think to ask them my name.

Red Beard wouldn't know. Neither would the fat man. Nothing would come of it, though; only dead men were judged incompetent. Stupidity didn't count. Red Beard and the fat man would play rummy for another ten years or so until the fat man died of a heart attack.

I swung by Gilberto's office before I left the police building. The door was open; I stuck my head inside. Gilberto looked up from his work.

"I think you people would be doing yourselves and Willie Fargo a big, big favor if you found some way to take him out of circulation for a few hours."

"A big, big favor?"

"It could save his life." I took off before Gilberto had a chance to say anything more.

I had to choose between justice and the best interests of 300,000 readers who depended on a vigorous and independent *Seattle Star* each day. If I made a wrong move, either the readers would get screwed or Roy Hofstadter would have my rear up on a felony charge.

Sometimes life was no damned fun. I had lost Shay, now this.

I drove to the *Star* and settled in behind my typewriter. Shay was gone but Charley Powell was there with his feet on top of his desk staring at the ceiling. He looked my way and drew his left hand across his face.

"What do you have, John?" He looked weary.

I looked up from my typewriter. "I know who killed Wes Haggart and the two girls."

Charley took his feet off his desk. "Was Wes a Harry?"

"We've got a Harry all right, but it wasn't Wes. Wes Haggart was straight arrow as far as I know."

Charley Powell rose slowly, walked to my desk, and sat on the edge of it. He looked at the technicians installing VDTs on the far side of the city room. "In a week or so those fellows will be finished installing those things. I don't like it but I'll live with it. I've survived television and fake ice cream, I'll survive the truth. Who's Harry?"

I rolled another piece of paper into my typewriter. "How would you like to work for Tobias Lane?"

Charley blinked. "What?"

"I said how would you like to work for Tobias Lane?"

He said nothing.

"You'll have to trust me and help me. You have to believe that I know what I'm doing and if it doesn't work out, the *Star* will be owned by Tobias Lane tomorrow morning."

"What do I do?"

"I'm going to sit here and outline the whole story on this machine. I'll give you an original in one envelope and a Xerox in another. Let's see, it's two o'clock now. I'll be leaving in an hour or so; if I'm not back by four P.M. sharp, you're to take the original to Roy Hofstadter and have someone write a story for tomorrow's editions from the copy, with my by-line up front."

Charley Powell cleared his throat. "Am I to assume that you'll be dead in such a circumstance?"

"Yes. But I doubt if it'll turn out that way. Do not accept my word on the telephone that all is well. I must be physically present in the city room. Is that clear?"

"Clear."

"Now if someone calls and asks about the evidence in the envelope, you tell them I wrote one only, the original. Tell them you watched me write it and that I appeared nervous and in a hurry."

"Got it."

"It doesn't make any difference who asks you, your mother, the President of the United States, the Second Coming, me on the telephone. You stick with that story. One original, that's all."

"One original in an envelope." Charley took a deep breath. "Am I to assume you're playing a gambit of some sort?"

I grinned. "Pawn to queen's bishop four. Out there all by himself. We'll see how the Harry answers."

"I'd better let you get it on paper."

"It won't take long." I started writing. Deadlines are nothing to anyone who has ever worked for the wire services or for an afternoon paper. The words came in a tumble. In twenty minutes the awful truth was there. I sealed each copy in a separate envelope and made a telephone call.

A woman's voice answered.

"My name is John Denson. I'd like to speak to Mr. Balkin."

"I'm sorry, I didn't catch your name, sir."

"John Denson. Please tell him it's important."

"One moment, Mr. Denson."

"Hello, John." Harold Balkin seemed cheerful enough.

"I think I should have a talk with you in private, Mr. Balkin. I know who the Harry is."

There was a momentary silence. "Haggart?"

"No sir. You know better than that."

There was a longer silence. "Who then?"

"I've written the entire story on paper and given it to Charley Powell. Right now I'm less interested in justice in the courts than I am in justice for the city of Seattle. I'm willing to negotiate a settlement—out of court, as it were." My hands were trembling and I could feel my heart beating.

"You're sure about what you have?"

"I have physical evidence."

"Are you going to tell me you have the murder weapon?"

"No, I'm not going to tell you that. What I do have is motive, the Harry's fingerprints on Wes Haggart's payroll card, and the name of the go-between who recruited the hit man."

I could hear Balkin breathing on the other end. "I'm not sure when I could get together with you for a talk."

"No sense stalling, Mr. Balkin. You won't be finding Fat Willie, I've seen to that. It has to be now, this afternoon, or the deal is off."

I heard the tinkle of ice. Balkin was having himself a soothing four fingers of whiskey. "I don't understand what it is you're after."

"I want to make sure Tobias Lane doesn't wind up with a controlling interest in the *Star*. In return for that I'm willing to give the Harry a break."

"Then I think you're right: we should have a talk."

"One more thing, Mr. Balkin, Charley Powell has orders that if I'm not here in the city room by four P.M., he's to give the contents of the envelope to Roy Hofstadter."

"Come on up then. Have you ever been to Broadmoor?"

"No, but I'm sure the man at the gate can direct me to your house."

"I'll see you soon then."

"We'll have a nice chat." I hung up.

I gave Charley Powell the two envelopes.

"Is your pawn out there?" he asked.

"All by himself and I want to tell you, Charley, he looks splendid. A bit of a shock for my opponent but that's what I intended."

"Did someone set Wes Haggart up?"

"Looks that way to me," I said.

Charley Powell returned to his work of editing copy. I got into my Fiesta and headed for Broadmoor, where the very wealthiest of Seattle's wealthiest lived. John Anders didn't live in Broadmoor presumably because he wanted to maintain the illusion of being in touch with the people. His neighbor, Arlo Daw, didn't live in Broadmoor because he was a vulgar hustler. But Harold Balkin lived there, surrounded by wealth, private guards, and a tall fence made of thick steel. One didn't take a leisurely drive through Broadmoor. One was invited and behaved oneself and acted civilized or one was thrown out on one's butt.

Broadmoor was situated on the side of a hill facing the city. The interstate highway was on the west; Lake Washington was on the east. It didn't take me five minutes to arrive at the main gate.

23

THE GUARD THERE WAS LEAN and trim, all leather, brass buttons, and efficiency. "Yes, sir?" he asked.

"My name is John Denson. I'm here to see Mr. Balkin."

"Yes, sir, Mr. Balkin is expecting you. Just bear to the right here and the road will make a wide sweep to the left. Mr. Balkin's house is the large green one with the pond and the ducks in front. I can't imagine that you'd miss it."

I shrugged and the gate swung open, controlled electrically by the guard from inside his booth. I turned right as I was told. The road swung left, as the guard had said. He was right, it was tough to miss Balkin's house. It was impressive among the impressive. Several handsome mallard drakes were mingling among the white domestic ducks in the pond in front of his house. The pond was surrounded by maybe two acres of rolling lawn. There was a putting green at the far end of the lawn. The house itself, built on several levels, contained, I assumed, a full complement of swimming pools, saunas, and the rest, paraphernalia that should be enjoyed by the young but are affordable only by elderly men with paunches. Balkin had thoughtfully provided a small parking lot for his guests. If the rain in

Seattle has its drawbacks, it also has its benefits. The grounds of Balkin's estate were handsomely landscaped. It was a pleasant walk up the tiled walkway to his house, which was built with natural wood topped by a roof of thick cedar shakes.

I punched the doorbell. Mellow bells chimed. The door opened. Harold Balkin answered, wearing slippers and a smoking jacket with a velvet collar. A costume for a gentleman and a scholar.

And here he stood with an automatic pistol leveled at my stomach. Big, mean-looking sucker. A German Luger. Collector's item.

"Would you like a drink while we chat, Mr. Denson?"

"Certainly. I assume I go first. Are we alone?"

"First door there on your left. We're alone."

Balkin's slippers padded along behind me. Balkin's study was much the same as Anders's only there was more of it. And where Anders had had a pool table, Balkin had a billiards table. A matter of class. Publishers played billiards.

"I'll bet Fat Willie shoots pool," I said, and sat down in a soft leather chair.

"Yours?" he asked, bowing slightly, gun in hand.

"I drank whiskey at Tobias Lane's."

"Whiskey then." He scooped two glasses into a bin of ice and poured us each about five fingers from a bottle of Jack Daniels. "What did you learn from Tobias?"

"That he offered both you and your sister the same deal, triple your current investment converted into Lane stock and tenure as publisher guaranteed until you decide to quit. Ruth told him to stick it. You said you'd think about it."

Balkin settled into an easy chair of his own and eyed me down the barrel of the Luger. "So?"

"So you had an option to match any offer for your sister Ruth's stock. The trick was to get her to sell. What was called for was a sudden, shocking collapse in the *Star*'s fortunes. Nothing permanent, mind you, but something to wound Ruth, who is on the ropes financially."

Balkin smiled. "I still don't follow."

"Of course you do. The answer was a Harry. The paper would recover in time. By then you'd have tripled your wealth with stock in a growing newspaper chain and still be publisher. The problem is the Harry could really be only one man: Wes Haggart, the most respected reporter on the *Star* staff."

Balkin took a sip of whiskey. "You have a marvelous imagination."

"Not as good as yours. The county prosecutor, eager for the *Star's* support in his political career, had already told you about John Anders's girls. Lovely things they are, but perfect for blackmail. You led Hofstadter to believe he'd struck a bargain. The question was, could you force your sister's hand by exposing John Anders?"

"And the answer?"

"Probably not. The public would be titillated but wouldn't stop buying the paper. In fact, the reverse might happen. No, it had to be Haggart. I'm guessing about some of this but my bet here is that you told Wes about Anders's girls and he went after it like a shark."

Balkin looked surprised. "Why would I do that?"

"To set him up as a Harry on the make for any way to extort a few bucks—even from his own editor—or as a Harry worried that management was onto him."

Balkin smiled vaguely. I was right on the mark or so close to it that I had his blood racing. "Wes had unusual freedom in the city room. He didn't have to check in with Charley as other people did. He didn't have to have his stories okayed in advance. When he smelled something, he went after it. If there was a potential libel problem, he took it to the company lawyer on his own. That's how you found out about his salmon-fishing story. You know and I know that the government, the press, and business in Japan cooperate in ways that would be considered outrageous in the United States. A simple phone call to our friend Hashimotosan was enough to convince him that you were Wes Haggart and willing, for a small fee, to help the cause."

"Please, help yourself to some more whiskey when you feel dry, Mr. Denson." The pistol never wavered an inch. I was right on the mark.

"Then one lovely evening you used your passkey to get into the payroll office, where you checked Haggart's payroll card

179

and found he had the newspaper send his money to his checking account each month. With his account number in hand you began your donations of five thousand dollars each month—more circumstantial evidence that Wes was on the take. Haggart knew someone was trying to set him up; he simply put the money aside in a savings account which he didn't touch."

"And what about you, Mr. Denson? Why did I hire you if I was trying to set Wes Haggart up as a Harry?"

"Well, you hired me to uncover the circumstantial evidence you planted against Wes. After I told you at The Gazebo that Haggart had been scrounging through Anders's office, you had him murdered. The cops would find out that he had been banking an extra five K a month. A dead man can't explain that he didn't know where the money was coming from. Haggart didn't spend a nickel. All you needed was rumor made public."

"And how was it that I murdered Wes Haggart when I wasn't even in town? If you'll check, you'll find out I made a trip to San Francisco that day."

"Fat Willie Fargo is known to police reporters. He would be known to you. Fat Willie hired the hit man for you and no doubt murdered him afterward. Fat Willie also spread the Harry rumor to the newspaper and the cops, in case they were too dumb to get the point. All you had to do then was sit back and wait for the accusations that would knock the pins from under your sister."

Harold Balkin eyed my pawn and thought about my next move.

"You lose, Mr. Denson."

I think I stopped breathing. "How's that?"

"The police will have to put Fat Willie on the stand to prove their point." He shrugged. "Would you like to make a call?" He motioned to a telephone on an end table.

I called Gilberto.

"Did you people get Fat Willie on ice?"

"He's on ice all right, he's dead," said Gilberto. "Dead since early this morning. Somebody pranged him in his sleep."

I hung up before the confused Gilberto had a chance to say anything more.

"It would have been nice to have him on the stand, but I've got enough anyway."

If Gilberto was confused, Balkin was something more than that. He blinked once, like some great trapped lizard, but recovered quickly.

Without Willie, my opener didn't look so splendid. But I had to play the board. I looked impassive. Tried to, anyway.

"You say you have 'enough,' Mr. Denson. Exactly what do you mean by that?"

I grinned. "I told you on the telephone that I put the whole story on paper and left it in an envelope with Charley Powell. Well, that envelope also contains a written deposition, signed, witnessed, and notarized. Fat Willie spilled his guts. And as I said, unless I'm back in the city room at four o'clock, Hofstadter gets everything."

"How do I know you're telling the truth?"

"You don't. You've heard my story, judge for yourself."

Harold Balkin lowered the muzzle of his collector's item. "What is it you have to offer?"

I took a sip of whiskey. "One day, Mr. Balkin."

"One day?"

"A one-day head start."

"In exchange for?"

"In exchange for your selling your shares of the *Star,* all of them, to your sister, Ruth, for the sum of, say, one dollar."

"Roy Hofstadter will have your ass in jail for obstruction of justice and God knows what."

"He wouldn't do that." I shook my head. "Oh, no, no."

"You have remarkable confidence in Mr. Hofstadter's goodwill."

I grinned. "I don't have anything of the sort. It's possible for me to single-handedly put the squash on his ambition to become governor or whatever and he knows it."

"You?"

"Well, me and Councilman Daw, actually."

The collector's item resumed its level position. Balkin's hand trembled. "You're talking about me in Rio alone and broke."

"What about the girl from Ipanema and all that? I'm told the

181

women are lovely in Brazil. You could have yourself a nice estate."

"No deal."

"Pull the trigger on that thing and you lose. Charley has his instructions. No, you wouldn't be broke. You must have assets you can convert quickly into cash. All I want is for your sister, Ruth, to own a solid controlling interest in the *Star*. If I saw you in jail right now, the *Star* would suffer terribly in the next few weeks and Tobias Lane would gobble it up. The only loser in that brand of justice is the city of Seattle."

Harold Balkin said nothing. He stared at me with the pistol in his lap, leveled at my midsection. He stared at me but he didn't see me. If this had been the movies, I would have jumped him, maybe sent the Luger sailing with the side of my foot. Only problem was he had his finger on the trigger; startle him and I could wind up with a slug in my stomach. Subsequent reports of my death would not be greatly exaggerated.

"How do I know you won't double-cross me?"

That was a hell of a question. I wasn't sure I had a satisfactory answer. I smiled. "Friend, you're due for four counts of murder one. I hold the gun, not you. I call the shots, not you. You have to take what you can get; you don't have any choice. I'm giving you my word that I'll give you a day. I mean it. If you're smart, you'll take my deal. Shoot me now and you'll spend the rest of your life eating food out of tin plates and being bullied by degenerates. Your choice."

"No, Mr. Denson, I hold the gun." He shifted the Luger to his left hand and dialed the city desk with his right. "Charley, this is Harold Balkin speaking. John Denson left an envelope with you. Yes, that's the one. How many did he write? Are you sure? Okay, Charley, I want you to have a copyboy deliver that envelope to my home in Broadmoor; it's very important." Balkin listened to Charley on the other end. I could see his jaw muscles working off the nervous tension. "I'm the publisher of the newspaper, Charley, and I'm ordering you to have that envelope delivered. You don't take orders from John Denson. You're just a city editor and that's all you'll ever be. I'm the publisher, Charley, and you're playing with my football: I call the rules. You either deliver that envelope or you're on the street and I'll see to it that you stay there. Do you understand what I'm saying, Charley?" He listened again while Charley Powell followed my instructions. "I'm going to put Denson on the phone and you can decide for yourself what you should do."

He put the receiver against his thigh and switched the Luger to his right hand. "I want you to order Charley to send that envelope up. If you don't, I'll blow you wide open. I don't have anything to lose." He handed me the phone.

I shrugged. "Charley, this is Denson here. I want you to have a copyboy send that manuscript on up here."

"Fuck you, Denson," said Charley Powell.

Shay cut in from her extension. "What's going on up there, John?"

"I'm sorry you feel that way, Charley," I said.

"Are you being threatened, John?" Shay's voice trembled.

"Oh, I'm okay, Charley."

"Do what he says," said Shay. "For God's sake, do what he says!"

"I'd like to have Shay write my story."

"Hang up the phone," Balkin ordered.

"Where are you? Shall I call the cops?" asked Powell.

"No need." I hung up and looked at Balkin. "I told Charley that nothing—ordering, begging, pleading, instructions from the governor—nothing was to violate my order. I either show up at the appointed time or he throws you to the wolves."

Balkin swallowed.

"Charley won't give up the envelope, but he knows where I am. He might be tempted to send in the marines."

"Tell me how the deal would work."

I grinned. "Now you're talking. Simple, really. I show up at the city room and instruct Charley to put another two-hour hold on the envelope. You and I deliver your stock to Ruth with the proper transfer papers signed. When that's done you have twenty-four hours. You should have time to get to the bank this afternoon."

Balkin thought that over. "I'll swap you the stock for the envelope. The twenty-four-hour crap is out. You can have your newspaper. I'll have the evidence against me."

183

I shook my head. "Roy Hofstadter has his eye on me. No way I'll be part of whitewashing five murders. A head start's worth it if it causes Tobias Lane to fold his tent."

"The whole loaf or nothing." Balkin stared at the floor.

"Nothing, then. You're not making sense. You know and I know that Hofstadter will find the truth with or without me and with or without Fat Willie. He's already wondering about Lane's presence in town. He'll ask your sister the same questions I asked. She'll give him the same answers she gave me. He'll eventually come to the same conclusions; he's a jerk but he's not stupid."

Balkin slipped his feet out of the slippers and into a pair of loafers he'd left beside the chair. Then he backed to a closet, opened the door with his free hand, and slipped a gray herringbone jacket from its hanger. He was careful, although I wasn't going to try anything heroic. I don't like to bleed.

"I think we should go see Charley Powell," he said.

I looked at my watch. "I guess that makes sense; you have thirty minutes to go."

"We'll take my Mercedes; you drive, Mr. Denson."

He was polite, I'll give him that. He laid the keys on the billiards table and backed off while I picked them up.

"I would like you to get my raincoat from the closet there, please."

I did as he said. I turned around and there was a small penknife on the billiards table with a blade opened.

"Slit the bottom seam of the right-hand pocket with the knife, please, then stand clear of the knife and the coat."

Again I did as he said. "Better to hide your pistol, Mr. Balkin?"

He nodded. "It is still raining outside?"

"Was when I drove over."

"Good. Then shall we go?"

We went. The Mercedes was a lovely car. Neither of us said anything. We watched the windshield wipers soundlessly clearing the rain and listened to the hiss of the radials on the wet pavement.

"I think you're going to lose, Mr. Denson," he said at last.

"How's that?"

184

"Your reconstruction was accurate in most details, but I think you were guessing most of the way. And in one crucial aspect I think you were bluffing."

"And what was that?"

Balkin smiled but didn't say anything. His upper lip and forehead were wet with sweat. I wasn't much different. I could feel a trickle of sweat move from my armpit down across my ribs. Balkin wiped his forehead with the sleeve of his herring-bone jacket.

"I'll bet we smell like goats," I said.

"*Mano a mano,* eh, Mr. Denson?"

I parked the Mercedes in the *Star*'s parking lot with fifteen minutes to spare on my deadline. "The keys, Mr. Denson."

I gave him the keys. He slipped them into the good pocket of his raincoat. He slid the Luger into the pocket with no bottom and we took the long walk to the city room.

"A fitting day for this, what with the rain," I said. "A rainy day in Seattle."

"A fitting day."

185

24

CHARLEY POWELL HAD BEEN watching the clock and the door. He had his eye on us from the instant I stepped inside the city room. Shay and Bob Sander were at their desks, pretending to work.

Powell rose from his chair by instinct. Harold Balkin was the publisher of the paper and his superior. "Yes, sir, Mr. Balkin, what can I do for you?"

Balkin smiled. "I have a pistol here in my pocket, Charley."

Charley looked at me.

"He does."

"Denson gave you an envelope earlier this afternoon. I would like it now, please."

"I'm afraid I can't do that, sir."

"Would you rather I blew you in half, Charley?"

"He wouldn't in front of a roomful of people, Charley."

"Shut up, Denson!"

I saw Sander get up from his desk and drift out of the city room, looking distracted and distant as usual. Shay was on the telephone. I said, "I don't think so, Mr. Balkin. If you dictate a confession and give your holdings in the *Star* to your sister, free and clear, you can have the envelope."

Balkin smiled. "Of course. Why not?"

Charley Powell rolled a piece of copy paper into his machine, dated it, and looked up. This was no problem for Charley. He had taken thousands of stories over the phone in his time.

"I, Harold Balkin, publisher of the *Seattle Star* . . ." Balkin waited for Powell to finish the phrase, ". . . do hereby freely and of my own accord admit to having arranged for the murder of Wes Haggart, a reporter for the *Star,* by a man named Bill Morton, an underworld acquaintance of William Fargo. Mr. Fargo hired Mr. Morton for the sum of five thousand dollars. Mr. Fargo later murdered Mr. Morton for the sum of twenty-five thousand dollars. I murdered Mr. Fargo in his sleep. Circumstances apparently forced Mr. Morton to murder the two young women with Mr. Haggart; that was not part of the agreement arranged by Mr. Fargo. The murders were part of a plan to raise public speculation that Mr. Haggart was on the take, a rumor that would have crippled the *Star* momentarily and forced my sister, Ruth, to sell me her holdings in the newspaper. Under the circumstances I would like to sell my holdings to my sister, Ruth, for the sum of one dollar so as to avoid the possibility of the *Star*'s falling under the management of a newspaper chain. Mr. John Denson, acting as my sister's representative, has this day paid me the one dollar. Will that do, Mr. Denson?"

I knew I didn't stand a chance of making it out of the building with that paper, but what the hell. "Sure, if you sign it."

Balkin smiled and signed. "My dollar, Mr. Denson?"

"Why not, I like games." I slipped my wallet from my hip pocket and gave him a buck.

"Now my envelope, Mr. Powell."

Charley looked at me.

"A deal's a deal, Charley."

Charley opened a desk drawer and pulled out the envelope containing the original of my document.

"Open it, Mr. Powell, and fan it across your desk like you might a hand of cards."

Charley did as he was told.

Balkin grinned. "Just as I thought, Mr. Denson, no affidavit from Fat Willie. Put it back in the envelope, Charley, together with my confession."

Charley looked at me again.

"You'd better do as I say, friends; I don't have anything to lose."

"Go ahead, Charley."

Charley went ahead.

"Now I want the both of you to come with me. Just be casual."

I saw Shay watching us as we left. She looked like she was ready to pass out. We strolled casually across the parking lot to Balkin's Mercedes. He had Charley get in the rear seat and he took the passenger's side. I was to drive. Only problem was the Mercedes wouldn't start. The engine ground but nothing happened. I tried it again. Nothing.

"Pump it once."

I pumped and tried again. Nothing.

The awful truth came to Harold Balkin. "Out, out, both of you! Charley, you get your car and get back here in thirty seconds or your friend Denson is minus a head!"

Charley scrambled out of the back seat and took off across the lot on a dead run.

I got out and saw the cop. Bob Sander had called the police. The cop had a pistol. I dove left and began tumbling and twisting across the asphalt. I heard Balkin's pistol go off once, twice. I was behind a Volkswagen bus. I looked and the cop was on the pavement in a spreading pool of blood. His pistol was five feet away from him on the pavement. Balkin had his pistol trained on the cop.

It was then that I did a foolish thing.

I sprinted from behind the bus, scooped the pistol in the direction of the fallen cop, and kept going. Balkin fired once but nothing happened.

188

I had refuge behind a Honda the second time around. I turned and saw Balkin staring at the cop, frozen.

The cop was not a he; he was a she, a young woman with auburn hair that had been tucked up under her police hat. And there, mingled with the growing pool of blood beneath her, were her intestines, sprawled like a tangle of enormous white worms.

But the cop had her pistol now, left hand gripping the wrist of her right as she had been trained in the academy.

"Drop it," she said evenly. Her pistol was steady.

A steam rose from her intestines in the cold Seattle air.

The muzzle of Balkin's pistol moved slowly in the direction of his temple.

"Drop it," she said. She seemed oblivious of the fact that her innards were flowing onto the parking lot.

I don't think Harold Balkin had any intention of dropping it. I don't think he was going to use it on the young woman, either.

But I didn't get the chance to find out.

In that one brief, ambivalent, uncertain moment, Charley Powell's fifteen-year-old Plymouth sedan came screaming out of the interior of the lot, smoke rolling from the rear tires, and he flattened the publisher of the *Seattle Star* with a sickening thud. I could hear the gears grind as he tried to force it into reverse for another pass over Harold Balkin's corpse.

"Don't do it, Charley. No, no," I yelled, and sprinted toward Balkin's body. Charley turned the Plymouth off.

"Stand back, stand back," the woman cop yelled at me.

I stood back. In ten seconds it looked like the entire police force of the city of Seattle had descended on the *Star*'s parking lot.

Charley Powell, city editor, stood wavering slightly, looking at the crumpled and bleeding body of Harold Balkin. A man whose job it was to excise bullshit and bad grammar had killed a man. He leaned against the trunk of his Plymouth, breathing heavily. Murders are what happened out there, in the street. Charley's concern had been whether his writers reported the snuffed-out lives in crisp, accurate leads.

189

"Good Christ, Denson, what have I done? I've killed a man."

What had he seen over the hood of his old Plymouth? Just Harold Balkin, a man responsible for the deaths of five people out of sheer, outrageous greed? Or was it more than that? Was it the whole world gone nuts? Was it the dazzler who had lured Shay to Los Angeles and show-business journalism? Was it the computer expert named Clifford arriving with his machines to rob the *Star* forever of a rich and storied past?

A good thing Wes Haggart wasn't alive to cover the incident. He would have asked questions that maybe didn't need asking.

"I've killed a man," Charley Powell said again.

"I know."

"I wanted to back over him."

"I know that too."

Bob Sander was suddenly there with the distributor cap from Balkin's Mercedes in his hand. "Hey, it's okay, Charley," he said.

But Charley Powell wasn't okay. I knew it and Bob Sander knew it; Sander looped his arm around Charley and took him by the shoulder. "Nothing else you could do, Charley."

A crowd had gathered in the parking lot. It was a hell of a show for open-mouthed gawkers: there was Harold Balkin's broken body, a nervy lady cop calmly talking to a fellow cop while her intestines oozed and spread, and Charley Powell on the verge of weeping. One of the woman cop's colleagues, a black man, left her and came over to me. "Maureen wants to thank you for retrieving her pistol for her. I'm told you're a private—why didn't you use it yourself?"

"It's a cop's business to shoot people."

"Did you know it was a woman cop when you scooped her the piece?"

"No."

He grinned. "Would you have done the same thing if you'd known?"

"Sure."

The cop stepped aside for the ambulance that was backing into the lot to pick up Maureen. "Listen, if your friend hadn't creamed that dude with his Plymouth, Maureen would have cut him in half."

An attendant scooped Maureen's intestines back into her body cavity with his hands and turned her onto her back. She was ghastly pale when they slid her into the rear of the ambulance. She had freckles and a small nose.

After the cops were finished with us, Bob Sander, Shay, and I went out and got drunk. The next time I saw Maureen was at the inquest into Harold Balkin's death. Maureen looked at me from the witness stand. We shared a secret, she and I. We both knew Harold Balkin was about to blow his head off when Charley flattened him. Neither of us said anything. What good would it have served? Roy Hofstadter asked the questions and I suspect he knew something was left unsaid. But he didn't pursue it because Maureen had been lying there with her intestines spilled on asphalt. Turned out she had a last name, Petersen.

About three weeks later, I received a package from Ruth Balkin, then owner and publisher of the *Seattle Star*. In the package was her soapstone loon and a check for $10,000. I didn't have any reservations about banking the check; I'd earned it. When Maureen Petersen was well enough I conned her into helping me spend some of it in Mazatlan.

It wasn't long after that when I saw Shay on the tube. The network had picked up one of her stories for the national news. It was a modest report on lesbian weddings in Los Angeles. There was Shay, interviewing young women in traditional wedding gowns, pretending it was all very natural, alternate sexual preference and all that. I sighed and turned off my set. I hoped Charley Powell hadn't seen her. I couldn't imagine that he had. Charley didn't watch television. He read history. Me, I had a jug of screw top, a head of cauliflower, and a paperback thriller.

Young men used to go to newspapers to know about life. They believed truth was necessary. Some were bewildered by what they found. Some were amused. Others were moved to contempt, to scorn, to rage.

H. L. Mencken was once asked why he hung around the

191

newspaper business if the stupidity of the country was so barbarous. He said for the same reason people go to the zoo.

I finished my book in about an hour, grabbed my darts, and drifted on down to the Pig's to watch the zoo and throw a few.

– 30 –